SPECIAL MESSAGE TO READERS

This book is published under the auspices of

THE ULVERSCROFT FOUNDATION

(registered charity No. 264873 UK)

Established in 1972 to provide funds for research, diagnosis and treatment of eye diseases. Examples of contributions made are: —

A Children's Assessment Unit at Moorfield's Hospital, London.

•

Twin operating theatres at the Western Ophthalmic Hospital, London.

•

A Chair of Ophthalmology at the Royal Australian College of Ophthalmologists.

•

The Ulverscroft Children's Eye Unit at the Great Ormond Street Hospital For Sick Children, London.

You can help further the work of the Foundation by making a donation or leaving a legacy. Every contribution, no matter how small, is received with gratitude. Please write for details to:

THE ULVERSCROFT FOUNDATION,
The Green, Bradgate Road, Anstey,
Leicester LE7 7FU, England.
Telephone: (0116) 236 4325

In Australia write to:
THE ULVERSCROFT FOUNDATION,
c/o The Royal Australian and New Zealand
College of Ophthalmologists,
94-98, Chalmers Street, Surry Hills,
N.S.W. 2010, Australia

THE MANHUNTERS

Young cowboy Clu Marvin finishes a cattle drive in McCoy and sets about enjoying his pay with some pals. But Sheriff Dan Brown has spotted Marvin's resemblance to the outlaw the Reno Kid . . . Soon, Brown and his corrupt boss, Lex Reason, plan to snatch Marvin and use him to claim the reward for the Reno Kid. Desperately, Marvin attempts to escape from the deadly duo. What follows is a bloodbath, leaving Marvin riding for his life — hotly pursued by the manhunters . . .

DEAN EDWARDS

THE MANHUNTERS

Complete and Unabridged

LINFORD
Leicester

First published in Great Britain in 2005 by
Robert Hale Limited
London

First Linford Edition
published 2006
by arrangement with
Robert Hale Limited
London

British Library CIP Data

Edwards, Dean
The manhunters.—Large print ed.—
Linford western library
1. Western stories
2. Large type books
I. Title
823.9′14 [F]

ISBN 1–84617–394–9

Published by
F. A. Thorpe (Publishing)
Anstey, Leicestershire

Set by Words & Graphics Ltd.
Anstey, Leicestershire
Printed and bound in Great Britain by
T. J. International Ltd., Padstow, Cornwall

This book is printed on acid-free paper

Dedicated with thanks to
actor and cowboy, James Drury,
who is truly 'the real McCoy'

1

Few can imagine what it would be like to be mistaken for a deadly outlaw with a $10,000 bounty on his head. To be confused with the ruthless Reno Kid and wanted dead or alive. To have the guns of justice aimed and fired at you with one single intent: to kill you. Not for anything you had done, but to lay claim to the price that had been placed on the head of the outlaw for whom you have been mistaken.

What man could cope with being hunted like an animal until he could no longer find refuge or sanctuary anywhere?

So it was for Clu Marvin.

The twenty-two year old cattle puncher and drifter had never even been arrested for drunkenness, unlike most of his fellow trail drivers. He had never even fired his ancient Colt .45 in anger since he first hired on to guide steers to the railheads of McCoy at the tender age of twelve.

Yet he fitted the description and crude photographic image which emblazoned the Wanted poster. A poster which promised the person who brought in the Reno Kid dead or alive the fortune of $10,000 in cash.

How many innocent men would fall prey to the eager bullets of those who wished to lay their greedy hands on the princely sum? A sum of money so great that it would see most men through the rest of their lives easily.

At first it had been something which had amused the young Marvin. Something which caused his fellow cowboys to tease him when they first spotted the poster pinned to the notice board outside the sheriff's office. He had laughed as heartily as the rest of them at being the double of someone so infamous. The innocence of youth and a naïve, trusting nature were no defence against those who could and would try and exploit such a situation. Marvin would soon understand that simple fact.

The sixteen cowboys had just been paid off at the McCoy auction pens after bringing a thousand head of longhorn steers over 300 miles up from Texas. They had done their job well and been rewarded.

Every one of the cowboys had earned the twenty-dollar bonus they had been paid on top of their wages and were headed for the main street to trawl the many saloons they had grown to regard as second homes. They were only yards from the railhead stockpens when they first noticed the sheet of bleached paper and its blurred image pinned to the notice board outside the office of Sheriff Dan Brown.

The Reno Kid had managed to achieve an almost cult status by robbing banks, trains and almost everything else a man could rob without ever being captured. Yet it was the killing that had raised the bounty on his head far above that for the less deadly thieves who plied their trade west of the Pecos.

The Kid had no conscience and would use his deadly skills to destroy anything that got in his way. Women and children fared little better than armed men when it came to becoming notches on the wooden gun-grip of his lethal six-shooter.

The outlaw had become a serious problem and embarrassment which the law had decided to eliminate at the earliest opportunity. But there was only one sure way to get the better of troublesome outlaws and that was to put a price on their heads which would tempt even their kinfolk.

With the help of rich bankers and businessmen back East the authorities had achieved their goal and raised the huge bounty. Thousands of freshly printed posters had been rushed from Dodge City to every town along the railroad tracks. It was important to the powers that be to stop the Reno Kid as soon as possible before he turned his attention to the rich pickings of cattle rustling.

But the innocent Clu Marvin and his fellow cowboys had not realized what it might mean to him if others actually believed that he was the infamous killer he apparently resembled.

It would mean either facing those who wanted to claim the reward on your head or turning tail and running. A gunfighter would choose the former but a mere cowboy would have to flee.

Marvin had been standing on the well-shaded boardwalk outside the sheriff's office with a half-dozen of his fellow cowpunchers when Sheriff Dan Brown stepped through the door and growled at them.

'Move on, you young galoots!' Brown ordered waving the aromatic cowboys away. 'Get to a saloon or a damn bath-house. You're stinkin' up my office and I don't wanna have to close the windows on account of no cowboys. It's hot and you boys are awful ripe.'

Four of the cowboys continued on

towards the closest of the saloons whilst Marvin and his best pal Toke Carter continued to study the poster.

'You deaf as well as smelly, boys?' the lawman shouted. 'Get your hides away from my office.'

Marvin smiled. He had turned to trail their companions when his sleeve was caught by Carter's outstretched left hand.

'Where you headed, Reno?' the ginger-haired cowboy joked.

The sheriff's wrinkled eyes narrowed as he gave Marvin a closer look.

'Hush up, Toke.' Marvin laughed. 'Some folks don't cotton to Texan humour.'

Carter grinned. He released his grip, hopped down off the boardwalk and started off towards the saloon.

'OK, Reno. I'm sorry. Don't ya go drawin' on me.'

'Hush up, Toke,' Marvin insisted.

'You better move or the sheriff will arrest you.' Carter laughed out loud before increasing his pace to catch up with the other cowhands who had already reached and entered the noisy saloon.

Clu Marvin turned his head and looked at the sheriff beside him. It was a stern expression the lawman returned to the smiling cowboy.

'Howdy, Sheriff. I'll get goin' before you have to stink up your jail by arresting me.' Marvin stepped down on to the sun-baked street and walked in his companion's footprints. Yet with every step he could feel Brown's eyes burning into his back like a branding-iron on a maverick.

'What's ya name, cowboy?' Brown shouted.

The cowboy looked over his dusty shoulder.

'My name's Clu Marvin, sir.'

'Of course it is, Kid!' Carter laughed.

Dan Brown rubbed his whiskered chin thoughtfully and turned to study the Wanted poster more closely. He then returned his eyes to the cowboy headed toward the saloon. A germ of an idea was taking root in his mind.

Toke Carter waited by the saloon's hitching rail and noticed the concerned look on his best friend's face.

'What's eatin' ya, Clu? You looks like ya lost a twenty-dollar gold piece.'

Marvin stepped up on to the boardwalk and paused. He looked over his shoulder again at the sheriff. Brown was still watching him the way an eagle glares down from a high thermal at its prey far below him.

'That sheriff seems to be looking darn hard at me, Toke. Kinda scares me.' Marvin swallowed hard. 'What you wanna go calling me Reno for? He might believe you.'

'Don't fret none,' Carter said patting the dust-caked cowboy. 'They're all like that. They see trouble in everyone. Reckon he thinks you're a bad 'un.'

Marvin smiled.

'He don't know me very well, does he.'

Both cowboys entered the saloon. Their wages and bonus money were burning a hole in their pockets. They had a thirst that had to be quenched.

As Marvin led the way through the swing-doors a cold chill traced up and down his spine. He shook and rubbed his neck nervously.

'What's wrong, Clu?' Carter asked as they inhaled the stale tobacco smoke which almost managed to conceal the heavy odour only hard-working men can create by simply being alive.

Marvin looked at his pal.

'I don't know. I just had me a feelin' someone walked over my grave.'

'You're just dry and tuckered like the rest of us worthless cowpunchers, Clu.' Carter laughed. 'A bottle of whiskey down your throat will cure that.'

The two men made their way through the forest of people until they eventually located the long, wet bar counter and the rest of the well-liquored trail crew.

'There he is, boys!' Pete Potter, the trail-drive cook roared out loud. 'The Reno Kid! Damn if I ain't scared!

Don't ya go shootin' up the place now, ya hear?'

'Hush up, Cookie,' Marvin shouted above the laughter.

One of a pair of well-pomaded bartenders strolled up to the two cowboys and stared at them.

'What'll it be?'

'Whiskey!' Toke Carter raised his voice above the din. 'A bottle!'

Marvin rested both hands on the bar and stared at the countless water-marks that had accumulated over the years. He glanced at Carter.

'That sheriff sure gave me a darn strange look.'

'They always do that,' Carter responded. 'They just try to scare ya. That way you won't do nothin' to get yourself locked up. Sheriffs are lazy coots. They don't wanna fight nobody if'n they can avoid it.'

'You sure that was why he looked at me so funny, Toke?'

'What other reason would he have?' Carter shrugged as the bartender placed the bottle before them with two thimble glasses.

'That'll be two bucks!' the humourless man shouted.

'Two bucks?' Carter complained. 'How can you charge that much for rotgut whiskey? You probably makes the stuff in the cellar for all we knows.'

'We ain't got a cellar.' The man inhaled and almost doubled the size of his chest. 'Do ya want it or not?'

'Sure we do.' Carter placed two silver dollars down and watched the man's hands expertly scoop them up. 'But how come you charge so much?'

'You just bin paid off, ain't ya?' The bartender smirked.

'Yep.' Both cowboys replied at exactly the same time. 'So what?'

'The boss always doubles the price of whiskey when a trail drive comes into town,' the man explained. 'It's called business, boys.'

'Daylight robbery would be a better description.' Marvin smiled.

The bartender ignored the statement

and moved along to the next thirsty customers.

Carter poured two shots and handed one of the glasses to his friend.

'Drink up, Clu. Maybe later we'll find us a couple of soiled doves and do us some courtin'.'

Marvin sipped at the whiskey and blinked hard. His eyes started to water as he coughed.

'Reckon you was right about them makin' this stuff themselves, Toke. I never tasted anything like this before.'

Carter opened his mouth and downed his drink with one swift movement of his right hand. He stared at the sawdust-covered floor for a few moments as the liquor burned its way down inside him.

He then stomped on the floor three times and looked up at the face beside him.

'Horse liniment with just a dash of iodine, I'd say. Smooth though. Darn smooth.'

Both men laughed. Marvin only

stopped when he caught sight of the sheriff's reflection in the long mirror behind the bar. The cowboy turned and looked over the heads of the rest of the saloon's patrons at the grim-faced lawman holding on to the swing-doors with either hand.

'Look, Toke. It's that darn sheriff again. He's lookin' right at me.'

Carter carefully filled his glass and then stared at the saloon doors.

'He's just checkin' that there ain't no trouble in here, that's all. Relax.'

Marvin ran a finger along the inside of his bandanna nervously and swallowed.

'He's lookin' at me, I tell ya. Straight at me.'

'Why would he do that?' Carter asked as he downed another shot of the whiskey and winced. 'Of all the cowpunchers on the drive, you are the most innocent-lookin' of us all. You looks more like a choirboy than a cowhand. Why would he be interested in you, Clu? Why?'

Clu Marvin felt uneasy and returned the intense stare back at Brown.

'I wish I knew, Toke! I sure wish I knew!'

The wish would be granted far sooner than either of the trail-weary cowboys could ever have imagined. For Sheriff Dan Brown had a plan hatching in his fertile imagination that would change Clu Marvin's life for ever. It would have little to do with truth or honesty or any of the other things elected law officers are meant to hold dear. It had to do with money.

Blood money!

* * *

As darkness descended over the sprawling cattle town of McCoy and a thousand oil-lanterns were lit along its busy streets and avenues, one man moved silently through the shadows of the back alleyways like a rat seeking the filth that had spawned him. Sheriff Dan Brown had only been in office for six months, after winning a very dubious election. A man more likely to collect and pocket large fines than to uphold the law and protect the town's citizens, Brown looked every inch the classic image of a frontier lawman.

Large by any standards, with drooping moustache and long unkempt hair that hung from beneath the large ten-gallon hat, Brown instilled fear into anyone who looked at him. A gunbelt strapped beneath his beer-belly held three holsters. A Colt Peacemaker .45 on his right hip balanced by a Remington New Model Army .44 on the left were not unusual in themselves, but it was the third holster near his left one with the Starr Double Action Army .44 that caught the eye.

Brown was a walking arsenal. A one-man army who knew his office allowed him to kill without fear of ever being charged with anything other than upholding the law. That had made him dangerous. For it was not the law or people of McCoy that benefited, but

Brown himself and those who had used their money and power to get him the job in the first place.

What the burly loud-mouthed man had done before arriving in the thriving McCoy, was open to question. Yet it was a question that would never be answered. For the truth was the man who wore the sheriff's star was as dark as the alleyway he moved along. He had lived his entire life as a hired killer before being enlisted to run for office in McCoy. A change of name had ensured that his past would remain undiscovered.

Brown pushed his way through a narrow break in a tall fence and walked up to the rear door of one of the town's largest houses, a red-brick structure which had been paid for with tainted money collected by the corrupt lawman. Yet this was not his home, it belonged to the man whom even he feared.

The sheriff looked over his shoulder to ensure that he had not been followed and then knocked three times. He waited until he heard the heavy footsteps through the solid oak door. A series of bolts were slid across from top to bottom before the door was opened a mere few inches.

'Who is it?' the voice of the massive bodyguard asked as he trained the barrel of his Colt on the sheriff.

'It's me. Dan Brown. Let me in, you fool.'

The man pulled the door open and allowed the sheriff to enter the large marble-floored kitchen. Brown paused as he heard the door being closed and then locked.

The bodyguard moved like a bear past Brown and led the way through the dimly illuminated corridors until they reached the only brightly lit room in the entire structure. A well-fed fire in a hand-carved marble setting kept the room well lit as the thin figure of Lex Reason strolled around with a glass of brandy in his left hand.

'It's Brown, Mr Reason.'

Reason glanced at the lawman with a look of surprise etched on his skeletal features. He nodded and gestured to one of the handsome chairs.

'Take a seat, Dan.'

Brown moved across the room and sat down. He removed his hat, placed it on his knees and stared up at the strange figure who seemed troubled by his unexpected visit.

'I had to come and talk with you, Mr Reason,' he stammered.

'I have told you not to call on me, Dan,' Reason answered. He sipped at his brandy and walked towards his uninvited guest. 'I have made it clear that it is not wise for us to risk people knowing that we are known to one another. This had better be good.'

'It is good, Mr Reason. Darn good!' There was a hint of excitement in the law officer's voice.

Reason stopped walking and cupped the crystal tumbler in his hands. He looked down at Brown. If the words had interested him, it did not show in his poker face.

'You know how I work, Dan,' Reason whispered. 'I deal in profitable enterprises. Making you sheriff of McCoy was costly yet it has rewarded me greatly for my investment. Is there a profit in this for me?'

'Yep!'

'Explain.'

Sheriff Brown inhaled and licked his dry lips.

'Major Seth Provine brought in a herd of steers earlier today from Texas. He had about a dozen and a half cowboys with him and one of them cowboys could mean big money to us.'

Reason took another sip of his drink.

'How could a cowboy make any money for us, Dan?'

'It's his face!' Brown gushed.

The thin man sat down opposite the sheriff, leaned back in his chair and crossed his legs. His curiosity had been aroused.

'Now I'm interested, Dan. How could the face of a cowboy possibly be worth money to either of us?'

Brown reached into his inside coat pocket, pulled out the folded Wanted poster and tossed it across the distance between them. It landed on Reason's lap.

'A scrap of paper? It gets even more intriguing.' Reason rested his glass on the arm of his chair and slowly unfolded the poster. His eyes looked at the blurred photographic image and then read the bold words. 'I do not understand. Is this cowboy the Reno Kid?'

'I don't think so,' Brown replied.

'Then how can we make money?'

'This cowboy looks just like the picture on the Wanted poster. He's the spittin' image of the Reno Kid, Mr Reason.'

Suddenly it dawned on the thin man what Brown was trying to say.

'I understand. The Reno Kid is worth ten thousand dollars dead or alive.' Reason smiled at the sheriff wryly. 'And all we have to do is make the authorities think the cowboy is him. Then the cowboy is killed and we claim the reward. Right?'

'Yep!'

Lex Reason rose from his chair with his own glass in his hand. He walked to the impressive drinks cabinet, poured out a glass of brandy, then returned to Brown. He handed it to the smiling lawman.

'Cheers,' he said.

2

The dust-caked herd of well-liquored cowboys had soon drifted apart as they staggered from one saloon to the next in search of other things to spend their hard-earned money on. Clu Marvin and Toke Carter, however, remained together as they located the Silver Garter saloon half-way down the long main street. The aromatic pair of cowboys located two empty chairs by a card-table and rested their aching bones.

They were both the worse for wear, but still capable of ordering yet another drink as they rested their elbows on the green-baize table-top.

Both men smiled and then laughed.

'What ya laughin' at, Clu?'

'Same as you, I guess,' Marvin replied.

'But I don't know why I'm laughin'.'

'Me neither.'

'You order two whiskeys, boys?' a female voice asked as a tray was placed down on the table's surface.

Both cowboys looked up. Not even a bellyful of rotgut whiskey could disguise the fact that the bargirl had seen a lot more summers than either of them. Probably twice as many. Toke Carter leaned back in his chair and stared hard at the woman's face. It was well-painted and powdered beneath what could only have been a wig. No woman could ever have grown a real head of hair like that, he thought.

'Howdy, ma'am.' He smiled.

The woman pulled a chair across the sawdust-covered floor and sat down close to Carter. Her dress was low-cut and had probably once looked good. Now it was like her: faded and well used.

'You boys lookin' for a good time? I can satisfy two as easy as one.'

Both cowboys giggled boyishly.

'Reckon me and Clu might have us a

little energy left, ma'am.'

Marvin shook his head as he lifted the glass off the tray and placed it to his lips.

'Thank ya kindly for the offer but I'm kinda tuckered, ma'am.'

She touched Toke Carter's forearm and squeezed gently. 'Dolly can show you boys a real good time,' she said. 'You ain't ever going to find no girl as nice as old Dolly.'

Carter raised his eyebrows and looked across at his pal.

'It has been an awful long trail drive and we ain't seen us a lot of females since leavin' Texas, have we.'

Marvin grinned at his friend.

'Go and have a good time with Dolly, Toke.'

'Listen to your friend,' she advised.

Carter blushed.

'I'm not sure, Dolly. I ain't had me a lotta experience in love-makin'.'

She fluttered her eyelashes. They seemed to have been caked in something black that neither of the cowboys could quite come to terms with.

'I've a room upstairs,' she added.

'Hey, that's darn convenient, Toke. You can't turn Dolly down when she only lives upstairs.' Clu Marvin smiled.

Carter licked his lips nervously.

'Gosh, Dolly. You're a real sweet lady but I just ain't in the mood at the moment. Me and Clu here ain't finished our drinking yet. We have been a long time without a good drink and gotta lot of time to make up.'

'Don't have to be shy with me,' Dolly said, leaning forward to reveal her more than ample bosom. 'A man has needs and Dolly knows how to give her man a real good time. C'mon.'

Carter lifted his whiskey and downed it.

'I'm not sure, Dolly.'

She whispered a price into his ear.

'Interested?'

Toke Carter considered the price. It seemed fair considering she was well over the hill, he thought.

'How long would that be for, Dolly?'

She whispered again.

Carter raised his eyebrows even higher and smiled at the quiet Marvin.

Marvin sipped at his drink.

'You thinkin' about it, Toke?'

Carter carefully stood and allowed the female to lead him towards the stairs which led to several rooms. He glanced back at Marvin and shrugged.

'I'll meet ya here in an hour, Clu.'

'Or five minutes, more likely,' Marvin muttered under his breath. He watched Toke being led like a lamb to slaughter up the flight of stairs to the rooms above the belly of the saloon.

The footsteps came from behind the young cowboy and did not bother him at first. Then he slowly realized that someone had stopped directly behind him. Marvin heard the familiar and chilling voice of the sheriff over his right shoulder. His blood froze.

'I bin lookin' for ya,' Dan Brown said.

Marvin gritted his teeth.

'How come?'

The lawman ignored the question and responded with one of his own aimed straight at the back of the cowboy's head.

'What did ya say your name was again?'

Marvin twisted around and looked up at Dan Brown. He was an awesome sight to sober eyes, let alone those that were red with too much whiskey.

'Howdy, Sheriff.'

Brown bent over and looked right into the nervous young cowboy's face.

'Listen up. What's ya damn name?' he repeated.

'Marvin, sir. My name's Clu Marvin. Why you wanna know for?'

Brown smiled.

'You busy, Clu Marvin?'

'No, sir,' Marvin answered. 'I was just waitin' for my pal to finish his business upstairs.'

Sheriff Brown rested his fingers and thumb on the cowboy's shoulder. He had a vicelike grip that urged obedience.

'Get on your feet. We got us some business of our own to talk over.'

'What kinda business, sir?' Marvin asked.

'Get up, boy. I got me a pal that wants to meet ya.'

'OK! OK!' Marvin stood up and felt the firm hand move from his shoulder to the centre of his spine. He was guided out of the saloon into the street. For a few moments the cowboy stood on the boardwalk desperately searching for a familiar face amid the hundreds of passing strangers.

Then he felt the full force of the sheriff's power push him forward. He started walking once again.

'Keep movin', sonny,' Brown ordered before he dragged the ancient gun from Marvin's holster and studied it. 'You ever fired this thing?'

'Not often,' the cowboy admitted. 'Well, hardly ever.'

'Ain't ya ever heard of gun grease and oil, boy?' The sheriff kept pushing the youngster along the boardwalk. 'A gun in this condition could blow your own hand off if'n ya squeezed its trigger.'

'Heck, I ain't no gunfighter, I'm just a cowboy.' Marvin protested. 'The only time I'd have call to fire a gun would be to turn a stampede. I ain't never seen one so I ain't used the gun in years.'

'Keep walking!' Brown tossed the gun into a water-trough and pushed the palm of his hand again into the back of the cowboy.

'Where to?'

'You'll find out in due time.' Sheriff Brown continued to hit the back of the cowboy along the boardwalk until they reached the corner. Then Marvin felt his right arm being tugged until his whole body was walking away from the glowing street lanterns and store façades and up into the black shadows of a dark alley.

'I hope ya ain't gonna kill me.' Marvin gulped.

'I will if ya don't shut up!' the angry lawman warned.

'But I ain't done nothin' wrong, Sheriff,' Marvin insisted. 'Honest. I just finished a trail drive for Major Provine.'

'That old Yankee has given me a lot of trouble,' Brown brooded aloud. 'He don't cotton to paying taxes like most of the other trail bosses. Reckon I'll have to teach him a lesson one of these days.'

Terror swamped the cowboy.

What was going on?

Why had the sheriff singled him out?

Could it have anything to do with the fact that he looked like the Reno Kid? A thousand thoughts darted through his mind. None of them made any sense.

'The major has been darn good to me and the rest of the boys, Sheriff. He's a retired soldier. You know how tetchy they can get.'

Brown used the side of one of his boots and caught the back of the younger man's thighs.

'Shut up and keep walkin', cowboy,' Brown commanded.

Both men continued to walk further

and further into the dark alleyways behind the array of buildings. With each step, Marvin felt as if he were heading for his own funeral.

'Where ya takin' me?'

'You'll find out soon enough!'

'I don't understand, Sheriff. What's this all about?' The voice of the cowboy was becoming more strained with each step he took. 'I'm gettin' a mite scared. Nope, I'm getting darn scared.'

The lawman grabbed at Marvin's shoulder and stopped him. He then pulled the loose fence boards apart and pointed.

'In there, Kid.'

Clu Marvin obeyed and entered the rear garden of Lex Reason's magnificent home. The terrified cowboy knew that he was in trouble and yet he could not work out what sort or why the lawman had picked on him. He stood before the rear door and watched as Brown's large knuckles rapped on its shadowy surface.

'Please tell me. What have I done,

Sheriff?' Marvin begged for answers.

Then he felt the gun barrel against his neck.

'Shut up, cowboy. Before I blow ya damn brains out.'

Clu Marvin could hear the sound of hefty footsteps approaching the door from inside the massive building. His heart started to race as fear overwhelmed him.

'What is this place, Sheriff?'

'Shut up!' Brown cracked the gun across Marvin's neck. He staggered as pain tore through him.

The sound of the bolts being released chilled him to the bone as did the sight of the bodyguard when the door was opened wide.

'That you, Brown?'

'Who else ya expectin', fool!' the sheriff kept the cold steel barrel of the Remington pressed into the cowboy's neck as they entered. 'Tell the boss that I got him.'

'I can see that, Brown,' Lex Reason said from the dark corridor before them. He curled a finger and whispered. 'Bring him this way.'

'You heard him, cowboy,' the lawman growled into Marvin's ear. 'Move them feet.'

Clu Marvin tried to swallow but there was no spittle in his bone-dry mouth. He trailed the gaunt figure with the gun still pressed hard into his neck just above his bandanna.

If fear could sober a man up, then the staggering cowboy was no longer drunk.

3

The sun had only just managed to rise above the skyline when the Texan cattle-owner and trail boss walked from his hotel with two of his top hands at his sides. There was concern etched on all three men's faces as they rounded up the rest of their wranglers and cowboys outside the Silver Garter saloon. Red White had been a top ramrod for more than a decade and knew how to handle men as well as steers. Able Jones was his scout and a man of few words but quick to action. They flanked the tall elegant figure as he approached the weary cowboys.

Major Seth Provine was every inch the highly decorated cavalry officer even though he had been retired for more than a decade. His straight-backed figure bore testament to the fact that he had been trained at and then graduated from West Point long before most of the inhabitants of McCoy had even been born.

Yet the years had been good to the tall man. He concealed his battle scars well and refused even to mention his outstanding military conquests.

'Is this all of them?' Provine asked White.

'Yep,' came the reply from the tough ramrod.

The major eyed the faces of the dishevelled men. Most of them had still not managed to button their shirts. He knew every one of his cowboys and when one was missing it screamed out to him like a ancient siren.

'Maybe Clu's up in one of them hotel rooms with some female company, Red,' Provine suggested. 'He's of an age.'

'Not according to Toke, Major.' White sighed.

Provine looked at Toke Carter. The cowboy leaned against a hitching rail holding his head as all men do when they have consumed enough hard liquor.

'Talk to me, Toke. Where's Clu?'

Carter looked up. His eyes refused to open fully as the lids flickered heavily.

'He just disappeared, Major.'

'He didn't go with a girl?'

Carter smiled and tilted his head.

'Not Clu, sir. He never goes with females like I do. He don't cotton to payin' for their company or pleasures like me.'

'Toke left Clu in the bar here last night.' Red White pointed at the locked doors of the Silver Garter behind the cowboys. 'When he came back down from pleasurin' himself with old Dolly, Clu was gone.'

The major was troubled.

'How long were you up with old Dolly, Toke?' he asked Carter.

The rest of the cowboys all turned their heads and stared at the blushing youngster.

'About ten minutes, Major.'

The cowboys began to chuckle until

Provine raised his voice and pointed a finger towards them.

'This ain't no laughing matter, boys. This could be serious. Really serious. For all we know young Clu might be lying wounded or even dead in some dark alleyway.'

There was a hushed silence as Provine's men absorbed the wise but disturbing words. The major moved away with White and Jones at his side.

'Ya reckon Clu is dead, Major?' Jones asked.

Major Provine glanced at the scout.

'Find him!'

The tall man aimed his boots in the direction of the sheriff's office and marched towards it. Unlike most trail bosses who brought herds of well-fattened steers to the sprawling cowtown, the major did not relinquish his responsibility for his cowboys after paying them off at the end of a drive.

He would take them back to his ranch in the heart of Texas until it was time for the next cattle drive.

Seth Provine knew that Clu Marvin was not the sort to simply disappear without telling his friends where he was going and when he would return.

Yet Clu Marvin was gone.

Provine had first hired the youngster when Marvin was barely twelve years of age, only been a few months after he had set up his cattle ranch in the heart of Texas on its fertile ranges, having retired from a lifetime in the cavalry. Now, a decade later he had come to think of the youngest of all his cowboys as not just a hired hand, but a son.

But the signs were not good.

Provine looked over his shoulder and watched as Jones and White gathered up the cowboys into two groups and headed off in separate directions to start their search.

Secretly the major feared the worst.

He knew the vermin that hung around such towns waiting for the unwary cowboys who had just been paid for their hard labour. They were deadly creatures who would rather kill than do an honest day's work.

Was Clu Marvin dead?

Provine stepped up on to the weathered boardwalk and started vainly to knock on the locked door of the sheriff's office. Even though there was no answer, he continued hammering with a clenched fist. With every blow one question kept filling his thoughts.

Could Clu be dead?

It was something the major refused to allow himself to believe.

4

The small town of Dry Gulch lay a mere ten miles from the prosperous McCoy but they were worlds apart. Yet it might have been so different if the railroad companies had laid their tracks to the west of the wide river instead of the east. Some had said it was the deadly desert that had steadily spread like a cancer closer and closer to Dry Gulch over the years which had ultimately settled the surveyors' minds. Whatever the truth, McCoy had reaped the rewards whilst its smaller cousin had continued to die slowly under the blazing, unforgiving sun.

The blistering white-sand desert that spread up from the arid Indian territories seemed to have spread with each passing season and destroyed everything in its path.

Few if any men had ever ventured

out into the desert that destroyed everything it overran. Entire forests had disappeared as the hot sand had enveloped their trunks and sucked the very life from them. It was said that not even the Apache would go into the land of white sand.

For more than a decade the townspeople of Dry Gulch had seen the slow sea of white creep towards them. Yet the weathered buildings were still there giving shallow comfort to the sturdy residents who refused to let the elements get the better of them. A solitary hotel remained next to the telegraph office defiantly across from the handful of other wooden structures. Yet this was no place for the casual visitor to find anything except thirst and too few wells. It had seemed as if the closer the desert came to Dry Gulch, the less it rained. It was as if the clouds were afraid to defy the unholy sunbaked sand for fear of retribution.

Dry Gulch was a place where usually only the lost or the drifting were discovered, accidentally *en route* to somewhere more hospitable.

But there were always those who used its remoteness to their advantage. These were outlaws with prices on their heads who were neither lost nor drifting and had deliberately chosen Dry Gulch as the perfect place to keep out of public view whilst still remaining close to their paymasters in nearby McCoy.

A town that was too poor to employ any lawmen drew outlaws like moths to a flame.

Those that came thought nothing of killing and destroying anyone who stood in their way, if they were paid enough to do so, that was.

So it was for the four lethal outlaws who had remained in the small isolated town since their leader had been elected to the post of sheriff in the neighbouring McCoy.

They remained in Dry Gulch and waited for their next orders.

Their services had only been required three times since Dan Brown had won the rigged election. Three times they had been summoned by the short encoded message he had sent to them via the telegraph office next to the hotel.

Three deadly missions had been undertaken by the four skilled outlaws and they had shared in the profits with Brown and Lex Reason which their deadly handiwork had achieved.

It had been two in the morning when the telegraph operator had nervously knocked on their hotel room door with the small scrap of paper clutched in his sweating hand. He feared waking the occupants but these were not men who kept the same hours that normal people lived their lives by. They would drink and gamble through the hours of darkness and then sleep for half the next day, unless they had work to do.

Vern Booker had given the small telegraph operator the only tip he was ever likely to get. He had allowed the man to live and return to his small office unscathed.

The outlaw turned up the flame on the oil-lamp that stood in the centre of the table amid playing cards, coins and crumpled paper money. He then studied the words on the paper carefully before handing it to his three comrades.

Vern's brother Silas had been first to read the short message. Then he passed it on to Tom Snape and Pern Roberts.

'Look's like we got ourselves another little job to do for old Dan.' Vern Booker sniffed as he gathered up the playing-cards and carefully shuffled them.

'I'll get the horses ready,' Tom Snape said. He buckled his gunbelt around his waist and checked his weapons.

'Do that.' Vern nodded.

'How come we gotta stay in this damn town whilst Dan lives it up with Lex Reason in McCoy?' Pern Roberts complained as Snape left the room.

Silas Booker looked at Roberts.

'You got a hankerin' to get hung?'

Roberts plucked his hat off the table

and placed it on his head of well-greased hair. He sighed heavily.

'Dan's the sheriff there. How come we'd get hung?'

'There's also a lot of mighty smart folks there, Pern,' Vern interrupted. 'Lawyers and cattle agents who do a lot of travelling. Them folks would recognize us for sure. I don't want no dumb penpusher to shoot me in the back for the thousand bucks on my head. Do you?'

'Then how come they ain't recognized Dan?' Roberts retorted. 'He's worth more than any of us. They ain't figured that Dan Brown is really Three Gun Dan Johnson yet, have they?'

Vern Booker dropped the cards on the table.

'Not as yet.' He smiled. 'But I reckon they will. That stupid shooting rig he's got is bound to jog some varmint's memory one day soon. Who else wears three damn guns?'

Silas Booker picked up his single-shot Springfield rifle and box of shells.

He was an expert with the long-range weapon and had managed to keep many a posse at bay over the years. He trailed the two men from the room and down along the dark corridor towards the top of the stairs.

'Did I read that message right, Vern?'

'What did you make of the code?'

'Did Dan say we've gotta pretend to be bounty hunters and kill the Reno Kid?'

Vern Booker nodded.

'That's what I read. You must be right.'

'Is Dan loco?'

'Us go up against Reno?' Roberts asked nervously. 'What's Dan trying to do? Get us all killed?'

Vern Booker led the men through the door and out into the sand-covered street. The desert wanted this town and like a hungry living creature never stopped creeping over its boundaries. It was still hot even though the sun had set more than six hours earlier, and sweat poured from them.

Silas and Roberts watched Vern enter the telegraph office and waited for the few minutes it took him to send his return message to Dan Brown. Booker left the office, then checked his long silver-plated Peacemaker thoughtfully.

'You tell Dan that we're on our way, Vern?' Silas asked cradling his rifle like a babe in arms.

'Yep. I also told him that we ain't goin' to the secret meetin' place. We're headed to his house.'

'How come?' Roberts asked.

'I want me some answers, boy. I don't mind doin' his dirty work, but I ain't gonna commit suicide for nobody,' Booker growled. He slid the seven-inch barrel of his gun into its holster.

They watched Tom Snape leading the four powerful horses from the direction of the livery stables.

'Do you figure we looks like bounty hunters, Vern?' Silas asked his older brother.

'Nope. But then, the only bounty hunters I ever seen was the vermin who tried to get the drop on us. You and me killed all of them, Si. I ain't never set eyes on no livin' breathin' bounty hunter.'

Snape tossed the reins to his three companions.

'I don't like this, boys,' Snape admitted as he stepped into his stirrup and mounted the tall horse. 'Reno's a dead shot and has more notches on his guns than anyone alive. Mark my words. He'll use us for target practice.'

Vern Booker hauled himself on to his horse.

'Don't fret none, Tom. Before we do anythin', I'm havin' me a word with Dan. I ain't being sent on no fool's errand.'

The four deadly horsemen spurred hard and drove their mounts across the arid sand in the direction of the distant cattle town.

5

Hal Cartwright had been a deputy far longer than Dan Brown had been a sheriff and it showed. He had none of the flamboyance of the man who had somehow managed to get elected against all the odds, but he was a solid law officer who had forgotten more about the job than most men would ever learn. A few years Brown's senior, Cartwright had been kept on as deputy in a vain attempt to make the election result appear honest.

The deputy had spotted the anxious cowboys a quarter of a mile back as he had entered McCoy's main street. Instinctively Cartwright knew that something was very wrong. He quickened his pace and stepped up on the long crooked boardwalk which fronted a row of assorted buildings. He could also see and hear Major Seth Provine as the tall man hammered on the sheriff's office door.

'What in tarnation's wrong, Major?' Cartwright asked as he came up beside the sweating man. 'You looks like ya got the world's woes on ya back.'

Seth Provine glanced at the only lawman in McCoy he truly trusted. The retired cavalry officer faced the deputy and sighed as if relieved that he had at least found someone who might be able to help.

'Where's the sheriff, Hal?' Provine asked, focusing on the calm deputy beside him.

Cartwright pushed the brim of his Stetson off his face and raised an eyebrow.

'Darn good question, Major. More than likely he's still in his bed though. Maybe I can help you.'

Provine watched the man pull out a large key from his coat pocket and slide it into the door's lock. A loud click filled both men's ears as the deputy turned it.

'I've lost one of my boys, Hal,' the major said anxiously.

Cartwright led the taller man into the office and raised the green blinds to allow the morning light in through the grubby glass panes. He pocketed the key and then sat down.

'A bit early, ain't it, for you to be worryin' about losing one of your boys? The kid's probably with one of the bargirls sleepin' off a long night's adventure.'

Province leaned over the deputy and gritted his teeth.

'Not Clu Marvin, Hal. You know him, he's not the kind to pay for female company. He disappeared last night and I'm worried that he's met with an accident.'

'Where'd he disappear from?' Cartwright knew Marvin and most of the other cowboys who worked for the major. It did seem out of character for the youngster to do anything except sit and sip at the neck of a whiskey bottle.

Provine pointed out through the

open doorway at the Silver Garter saloon.

'From there.'

The deputy leaned forward until his elbows were resting on the top of the desk. He interlocked his fingers and ran a thumbnail along his bottom lip.

'And you're certain that none of the girls invited him up to her room?'

'My ramrod Red White checked it out. None of them ladies had any business with Clu, Hal.'

Cartwright rose back to his feet and strode to the side of the worried major. He rested a hand on the elegant man's straight back.

'Don't you fret none, Major. C'mon.'

Provine looked at the deputy.

'Where we going?'

'To the Silver Garter.' The deputy pulled the brim of his hat down until it shaded his vivid blue eyes.

'But the saloon is locked up now.'

Cartwright gave a low laugh as the sun flowed over them.

'They'll open up for me. They know

that I like nothing better than kicking doors off their hinges, Major. C'mon. I want to ask me a few questions myself.'

The two men stepped down into the wide dusty street and headed straight for the saloon.

* * *

There was an air of trepidation about the cowboy as he rubbed his wet hair with a towel before tossing it on to a chair and moving out on to the wide landing. Clu Marvin had never been so clean in all his days yet he was still confused by the situation he found himself in. None of the previous eight hours made any sense.

When someone drags you from a saloon, disarms you and then uses a gun to encourage you to go where he wants you to go, and then, when you are expecting to have your brains blown out, you are treated to a scented bath and an entire new wardrobe of clothes, you do wonder why.

Marvin certainly had good reason to be confused.

Maybe he was just too innocent fully to comprehend what his captors had in store for him. He had no knowledge or understanding of creatures like the suave Reason and the deadly Brown. He had only ever had the company of honest people in his short hard-working existence.

'Keep movin', cow puncher!' the bodyguard muttered a couple of steps behind the youngster. Marvin glanced back at the big man and did exactly as he was instructed. He kept moving towards the top of the opulent landing.

His eyes darted around the luxurious furnishings that adorned every square inch of the magnificent house. Drapes hung at every window with gold thread woven into their expensive fabric. The wallpaper had to have been shipped from back East to look so regal, he thought. Carpets beneath his bare feet felt so soft he had trouble balancing.

Oak and mahogany dominated everything from the long wide staircase to the hand-carved chairs and furniture which was everywhere he looked.

The cowboy knew that whoever the thin, strange man called Lex Reason was, he certainly had wealth and was not afraid to display it.

It was a wary Clu Marvin who walked slowly down the long carpeted stairs toward the spacious hall and the study beyond. Doors that stood at least twelve feet high were opened wide revealing the two men within its wood-panelled interior. They were watching him as he in turn watched them.

Marvin felt uneasy in his new outfit. The clothes were crisp and cleaner than anything he had ever worn before. He wondered why Reason would insist that he bathe and change from his well-worn trail gear into these expensive duds.

It made little or no sense to someone pure of thought.

The bodyguard trailed Marvin like a shadow and had done so since his boss, Lex Reason, had snapped his bony fingers early the previous night. The huge grizzly bear of a man, called simply Bruno, had no weaponry.

He did not need any. It was obvious even to the youthful cowboy that anyone built like that could kill anything he wanted to kill with his bare hands. Guns or knives would have been redundant in his charge.

'C'mon, Kid!' Brown growled as he rested the palms of his hands on two of his gun grips. 'No need to be nervous of me and Mr Reason.'

Marvin knew there was no truth in the words that dripped like a rattler's venom from the lips of the sheriff. He could sense the danger in the man with three guns strapped to his hips.

'He looks almost human now, Brown,' Reason said, pressing his fingertips together in a strange fashion as he studied Marvin with a keen eye. 'It seems a shame to waste such a creature for mere profit.'

The sheriff nodded.

'Reckon now he's scrubbed all that trail dust off his carcass and put on them fancy duds you got for him, he looks even more like the Reno Kid. I can almost smell the bounty money.'

'Be careful of your words, Brown,' Reason warned. 'We do not wish for our investment to flee just yet.'

The lawman sniffed.

'We could end this here and now and I could wire the authorities to get that reward money counted.'

'No! We stick to my plan!' Reason insisted.

Dan Brown scratched his whiskered jawline and silently nodded.

The thin figure of Lex Reason almost floated around the cowboy as he inhaled the aroma of the perfumed soap that had replaced the stench of trail sweat. His eyes darted all over the young man. It made Marvin even more nervous, although he could not understand why.

'I don't get this,' Marvin announced as he planted his bare feet firmly on the expensive carpet in centre of the study. 'I thought you was gonna kill me. You pokes guns in my neck and then you makes me take a bath and gives me new clothes. Nope, I don't get this at all. Can't you make up your minds what yo're gonna do with me?'

'You looks mighty worried, cowboy!' the lawman grinned.

Marvin's head turned.

'Yep. I'm worried OK. Darn worried.'

Lex Reason tapped his lips with his skeletal fingertips and continued to look the cowboy up and down as if inspecting a new possession.

'There's something missing, Brown. I cannot think what but he needs something else to complete the illusion.'

'What's an illusion?' Marvin asked innocently.

Reason ignored the question as he kept walking around the stationary figure before him.

'Boots would help,' Sheriff Brown suggested.

Lex Reason waved his hand in a dismissive way at the lawman and returned his attention to the nervous cowboy.

'I had boots sent over with the clothes. No. There is something he needs to set it all off. He still does not look like a deadly outlaw.'

'What ya mean by that?' the cowboy asked.

'A bandanna?' Marvin heard himself suggest without really knowing why.

Reason nodded.

'Yes. That would help. A red one, I think.'

Dan Brown exhaled loudly and shook his head.

'What about a fancy shootin' rig? I hear tell Reno has a darn nice one with a pair of matched Colts.'

Clu Marvin kept hearing the name of the Reno Kid being mentioned by the two dark-souled creatures and wondered why they might be trying to make him look like the infamous outlaw. He could not understand the motives of dishonest men.

Reason sighed heavily and walked to the drinks cabinet. He pulled the crystal stopper from a decanter and poured out three glasses of brandy. He took a sip and closed his eyes momentarily as if savouring the flavour as it made its way down into his innards.

'I have such a gunbelt and guns being delivered at any time. I sent Bruno to awaken the gunsmith whilst you were out. They ought to do just fine.'

Brown paced to the side of the gaunt man and lifted one of the glasses up. He downed its contents in one fluent action and poured himself a refill.

'Maybe a frock-coat?' the sheriff offered.

'Brilliant.' Reason smied. 'I can see him in it now. Black, I think with a felt trim on its collar. I have one upstairs which should do just fine. I think a black hat to match might just complete the transformation.'

'Reno wears a grey hat on the poster.'

'I say he wears a black one,' Reason insisted.

'OK. Black. I don't really give a damn.' The sheriff shrugged and walked towards the window. The sun had only risen an hour earlier and had yet to inflict its full strength on the red-brick building.

Lex Reason meandered to the side of the sheriff.

'Did you dispose of the cowboy's rags as I instructed whilst the young lad was bathing?'

Brown nodded.

'Yep. I scattered them filthy clothes around by the river just like ya told me. It'll make folks think that the cowboy drowned after taking himself a dip. Whiskey and swimmin' don't go together, do they, Mr Reason?'

'Indeed they do not. Excellent work.' The thin figure smiled. 'Now Clu Marvin shall be reborn as the Reno Kid.'

Sheriff Brown chuckled.

'Gonna be a darn short life, Mr Reason. If me and my boys have anything to do with it.'

'You have contacted them?'

'Yep. They're headed here as we speak from Dry Gulch. Goin' to meet me at my house,' Brown confirmed.

Reason looked troubled.

'Your house? Why not the secret meeting-place?'

Brown raised his shoulders.

'I don't know. Vern Booker seemed to be troubled about somethin'. You know what he's like.'

'He's dangerous, Brown.' The thin man exhaled. 'He'll ruin everything. I think that it might be wise if you ride out later and try to intercept them before they reach McCoy.'

'OK!'

Clu Marvin took a cautious step towards the two whispering men and cleared his throat. He could feel his heart pounding almost as hard as the war drums that still beat inside his skull.

'What ya keep talkin' about the Reno Kid for, gents? You know I ain't him, don't you? I just kinda looks a little like the critter, that's all. What in tarnation are you up to?'

Both Reason and Brown looked at one another and smiled knowingly. They did not answer the question.

'Do you like brandy, young man?' Lex Reason asked, changing the subject as he moved to the cowboy with two glasses in his hands.

Marvin raised an eyebrow. His head still hurt from the cheap whiskey he had willingly consumed the night before but the smell of the expensive amber liquor tempted him.

'I don't know. I ain't never tasted it before.'

Reason handed one of the glasses to the cowboy.

'Here. Try this. It is the best. French from St Louis.'

Marvin licked his lips and downed the brandy in the same manner that he had seen Brown consume his first glass.

He closed his eyes momentarily, then opened them wide. Tears rolled down his cheeks as the fumes enveloped him.

'That's good liquor.' He coughed.

Reason shook his head as if in despair and gave Marvin a long hard stare before turning to Brown.

'Polite society shall not mourn the loss of this cowboy.'

All of the men inside the study turned their heads at precisely the same moment as their attention was drawn to the large front door. Someone was knocking on its etched glass panels, sending an echo around the cavernous hail.

Reason snapped his fingers at the bodyguard.

'That'll be the gunbelt and weaponry, Bruno.'

The large figure moved like a well-trained hound. Clu Marvin turned on his heels and went to follow when Sheriff Brown hauled two of his pistols from their holsters and swiftly cocked their hammers.

The cowboy stared open-mouthed down both the gleaming barrels and swallowed hard. He trembled as the figure closed in on him until the cold steel was pressed into his face.

'Just make one sound and it'll be your last, Kid!' the lawman warned in a low whisper.

Marvin slowly nodded.

Reason walked past the two men when he heard the front door being closed once more and the heavy footsteps of his bodyguard returning.

Bruno held a large cardboard box in his hands. He entered the study and placed it on top of a round table. He stepped back as Lex Reason pulled the lid off the box and cast it aside.

'Is it the guns?' Brown asked, lowering the guns and releasing their hammers.

'Indeed it is. A finer set of matched Colts has yet to be made, I'd wager.' Reason sighed. His bony digits stroked the guns resting in the hand tooled holsters on the well-crafted belt. 'I dare say that the real Reno Kid does not have anything this good strapped around his hips.'

The sheriff strode to the side of the thin man and looked down at the weapons.

'Reckon you're right, Mr Reason. Them's fine guns and no mistake.'

Clu Marvin watched as the two men drooled over the contents of the box like vultures studying an animal about to drop. The cowboy was now sure he knew what they had planned for him. It seemed far-fetched that anyone would go to such lengths to have someone killed, but he had not considered the financial rewards their endeavours would reap.

Marvin had no idea that an investment of a hundred dollars on soap, clothes and guns could reap a $10,000 harvest.

The cowboy cleared his throat loudly and watched Brown and Reason look at him.

'You're gonna kill me, ain't ya? That's

what all this is about, ain't it?'

Lex Reason faced the cowboy.

'Why would we do that?'

'I ain't sure, but I reckon you must be gonna try. It has somethin' to do with this damn Reno Kid varmint you keeps talkin' about.'

'Tell me, dear boy. Do you sing to your cattle?'

'Now I ain't a violent critter, but I'm startin' to get a tad angry, Mr Reason!' Clu shouted at the thin figure.

Reason raised his right arm and snapped his fingers.

'Bruno!' he said.

Suddenly Marvin felt a powerful blow catch him across the back of his neck. He staggered and then fell heavily on the thick carpet at the feet of the two men.

'Well done, Bruno.' Reason smiled to the faithful and well-trained bodyguard.

Sheriff Brown rubbed his face. Even he feared the large man who obeyed every command Reason gave him.

'It'll have to look right, Mr Reason.

We can't just kill him here and then drag his carcass to the telegraph office and wire for the reward. Now it's light we're stuck with the varmint until sunset. Too many fluttering lace drapes in this damn street to do anything without witnesses.'

Lex Reason inhaled deeply.

'I know. We have to do this perfectly so that no one will ever realize what we have done. No one must be any the wiser to the fact that our little cowboy is not the real Reno Kid.'

The sheriff agreed.

'Yep. We have to get him out of town unseen and then let him ride out on the horse I've hand-picked for him down at the livery. I figure the nag ain't got more than a half-gallop in him.'

Reason grinned.

'And the Booker brothers and their two companions will then cut him down and bring him to you at the agreed place?'

'Damn right,' Brown said. 'And I'll appear to be collecting the reward money for the bounty hunters who just killed the Reno Kid. Hell, I gotta admit it, ya sure have a way of comin' up with dandy plans, Mr Reason.'

Reason smiled.

'Perfectly simple really. It is only business after all.'

'You think the real Reno Kid will get a tad upset when he hears that we collected the reward on him? He might come lookin' for us.'

'Ten thousand dollars buys a lot of protection,' Reason replied.

Dan Brown looked at the unconscious cowboy.

'How come I got me a feelin' we'll need every cent of it?'

6

There was and is an aroma which is unique to saloons. A mixture of stale beer, hard liquor, tobacco smoke and human sweat that lingers in the very fabric of the buildings themselves. Some even have the ghosts of cheap bargirl perfume added to the pot for good measure. No amount of scrubbing can ever quite defeat its powerful unseen presence. Most saloon proprietors know that merely sweeping out the well-trodden sawdust and replacing it with fresh is enough to satisfy their patrons. So it was with the numerous drinking-holes in McCoy. The Silver Garter was no exception.

Deputy Hal Cartwright was now sharing the fears and frustrations of the retired cavalry officer. He sat at one of the numerous card-tables next to the largest of the saloon's windows and stared out into the still quiet main street.

Dolly and the rest of the bargirls could add nothing to what they had told Red White earlier. He tapped his fingers on the green baize and watched Major Provine brooding at the long bar counter.

'Folks just don't vanish, Hal!' exclaimed Provine.

'Maybe the barkeep will know somethin' more about young Clu's disappearance, Major,' the deputy said.

Provine looked at the reflection of the lawman in the mirror behind the pile of glasses and bottles.

'Do you really think so, Hal?'

'I hope so, Major. I sure do hope so.'

'Who owns this saloon, Hal?' the major asked curiously.

'The same critter who owns most of the businesses in this town. Mr Lex Reason, down on Maple Avenue. He's an Easterner by all accounts who don't ever come out of that big red house of his.'

'Lex Reason.' Provine repeated the name as if he knew it.

'Yep. Lex Reason. You know him?' the deputy asked.

'I'm not sure,' Provine muttered. He turned and looked at the seated deputy. 'It's an unusual name that seems to ring a bell. Where have I heard it before?'

'They say he's got more money than the bank,' Cartwright added. 'Ain't nobody who knows for sure though. He's a rich hermit.'

'Most men who hide away from prying eyes do so for a purpose, Hal,' the major noted. 'I'd like to get me a look at him for myself.'

'You ain't on your lonesome there.'

Both men heard the ruckus on the saloon landing and looked upwards. The surly bartender had been dragged from his bed by the females and was being ushered down the stairs.

'What's goin' on? Some folks don't get any shut-eye 'til gone four of a mornin'. Why ya waking me up for, Deputy?' The man staggered across the sawdust-covered floor towards the lawman.

Cartwright pointed at the empty chair opposite him.

'Sit down. I got me some questions to ask ya!'

The bartender snorted as he placed his rear on the hardback chair.

'What if I don't wanna answer no damn questions?'

Major Provine stepped up to the seated man.

'I'm not in any mood to play games, mister. You answer or I'll get angry. I promise you, it ain't worth the grief.'

The bartender looked up into the stern features of Provine and then across at Cartwright.

'You gonna let him talk to me like that?'

The deputy raised his leg and kicked out under the table with all his might. He caught the bartender across his left knee with the high heel of his left boot. The sound of a bone being cracked filled the large saloon. Cartwright watched as the pain screwed up the bartender's face.

'Argh!' the bartender screamed. 'What the hell did ya wanna go do that for?'

Cartwright slammed his fists on the table and leaned across at the man.

'I'll do a darn sight worse if'n ya don't answer our questions! Reckon ya know that I'm already angry. You ready to answer now?'

'OK! OK!' the man cried out. 'What ya wanna know?'

'There were two cowboys in here last evening,' the deputy started. 'One went up with Dolly and the other stayed right here at this table. What happened to the cowboy that was sat here?'

The bartender rubbed his face with his sleeve.

'Ya ain't gonna like it, Hal,' he said shaking his head and rubbing his leg feverishly.

'Like what?'

'The answer,' the man answered.

'Just tell me what happened,' Cartwright insisted.

'It was the sheriff. He come in here and leaned over the cowboy. Then I saw them leave.'

The deputy glanced up at Provine.

'I don't get it.'

'Did the cowboy go willingly?' the major asked.

The bartender shook his head slowly.

'Nope. I'd say that kid was scared. Darn scared. Sheriff Brown ain't a critter you wanna argue with, though.'

The eyes of Provine and Cartwright met. They knew that Dan Brown had something to do with the mysterious disappearance of Clu Marvin.

But what?

And why did the sheriff escort the law-abiding youngster out of the Silver Garter and into the night? There had to be a reason for it, both men silently assumed. Yet neither could work out what possible motive Brown could have.

The deputy stood up.

'You can get back to your bed, barkeep,' Cartwright said, waving the man away.

The bruised and shaken bartender did not require being told twice. He stood and limped away as fast as he could.

Provine rested a hip on the edge of the card-table.

'Where is the sheriff, Hal?'

'I ain't sure. At home, I guess.'

'Do you think he'd mind having a couple of visitors this early?' the major asked as his eyes followed the bartender up the stairs to the landing and the near-naked females who were hanging over its balustrade.

Hal Cartwright straightened his gun-belt and headed for the saloon's door.

'Let's go find out, Major,' he said. 'He lives over on the outskirts of town near the river.'

Both men walked out into the morning light, then turned and headed in the direction of Sheriff Brown's home.

They had only gone a hundred yards when Red White came running out from an alley with a few of the cowboys.

'Major! Hold up, Major!' White called.

Provine and Cartwright turned to face the cowboys. They could see the bundle in Red White's arms.

'What's he got, Major?' the deputy asked.

'Clothes,' replied the major. 'Looks like Clu's trail gear, Hal.'

White stopped beside the two men.

'I found these duds near the river, Major.'

Provine nodded slowly as his fingers inspected the garments.

'They're Clu's OK!' he confirmed.

The deputy's eyes narrowed.

'Show us where ya found them, Red.'

The men marched off through the alleyways, heading for the river. Their pace was faster now than before. Far faster. It was as if they knew that time was against them and they had to try and locate the lost cowboy as soon as possible.

'Down there, Major,' Red White said aiming a finger at the water's edge. 'That's where we found Clu's clothes. He must have bin liquored up and gone swimming. He must have drowned.'

The deputy realized something he had not even thought of earlier.

'I just thought about somethin', Major,' Cartwright said as the men moved over the rough ground and down towards the angry river.

'What, Hal?' Provine asked as they came to a stop next to the fast-flowing waterway.

'The sheriff's house is only spittin' distance from here.'

Seth Provine turned and looked at the rows of buildings above them.

'Which one belongs to Dan Brown?'

Cartwright pointed.

'That one.'

The major tilted his head and looked at his troubled cowboys and then Red.

'You're wrong about Clu going

swimming, Red. Dead wrong.'

'He is?' Cartwright asked.

'He sure is. Clu can't swim a stroke. He's scared stiff at even the thought of trying to swim. He'd never go anywhere near a river without a good horse under his backside to hang on to.'

The lawman rubbed his chin.

'This don't add up at all, does it.'

Provine stepped forward. He bit his lower lip as he focused on the four riders in the distance, heading towards McCoy.

'Look, Hal. Riders.'

Cartwright nodded. 'Heavily armed riders, Major. Look at the sun catching all their hardware. Whoever they are, they're loaded for bear.'

White screwed up his eyes.

'I know that lead rider. He's Vern Booker, the outlaw.'

'You sure, Red?' the deputy asked. 'Them boys are an awful long ways off.'

'Red has eyes like a hawk, Hal,' the major told him.

The deputy shrugged.

'You sayin' that's Vern Booker? You positive?'

'I ought to be, Deputy. He shot me once real bad.' Red spat at the ground.

Major Provine inhaled deeply.

'And by the looks of it, they're headed towards the sheriff's house if I'm not mistaken.'

Hal Cartwright looked at the ramrod and then handed him his office keys.

'Here, Red. Take the boys and run back to the sheriff's office. Get all the Winchesters off the wall rack and a few boxes of shells out of the desk. Then come on back fast. Me and the major are gonna go sneak up there and see what them *hombres* are doin' in McCoy.'

White and the cowboys did as they were told.

Cartwright led the major away from the river and up into the rough ground below the lines of houses.

'What you thinking about doing, Hal?'

'I ain't too sure just yet, Major. But

this whole thing is gnawin' at my craw and I just hate mysteries. We have to find out what this is all about.'

Suddenly both men stopped in their tracks and leaned into the shadows. Above them they saw another rider. He was heading out towards the approaching four horsemen.

It was Dan Brown.

7

'Easy, Major!' Hal Cartwright's tight hand gripped Major Seth Provine's forearm firmly and held him back in the shadows away from the rays of the unforgiving morning sun. They both watched the sheriff spur his horse into a gallop on the road above them. A cloud of dust flew up off the hoofs of the black gelding and drifted over the top of the brush where the two men concealed themselves. It floated down over the rough ground behind them towards the fast-moving river.

The two men stepped back into the sunshine.

'Now where do you reckon the sheriff is headed?' the deputy asked, resting his wrists on his gun grips.

The two curious men watched Brown head quickly away from McCoy through the trees in the direction of the four horsemen who were coming from the direction of the vast sandy desert.

It was obvious to both onlookers that the sheriff had advance knowledge of the outlaws' imminent arrival in the cattle town. The deputy and the major continued to watch as Dan Brown got further and further away from McCoy and closer to the outlaws. Then they lost sight of the rider as he rode down into a deep ravine that fringed the river. Brush and tall trees masked anyone who used that isolated route from prying eyes.

'Why did you stop me, Hal?' the major asked angrily. 'I could have made it up to the road and stopped him. Damn it, I could have dragged him off his horse.'

Cartwright rubbed his chin and eyed his companion. He was far calmer than his associate, yet no less troubled.

'Why would ya have wanted to do that, Major? If Brown is up to somethin', and I got me a gut feelin' he is, he ain't gonna admit it to you, is he.'

Seth Provine looked at the ground and kicked its loose surface. In all his military campaigns, he had never felt so utterly frustrated or helpless. This situation was totally alien to him.

'I reckon not. But I have to find out what's happened to young Clu. For all I know that man might have killed him and thrown his dead body into that river. Dan Brown must have some answers and I want them. Even if it means learning that Clu's dead, I have to know.'

'How do you figure on getting answers from a man like Dan Brown?' Cartwright said in a low voice.

It was a good question.

The retired cavalry officer sighed heavily. He knew that the deputy was right. Dead right. Men as tough as Dan Brown would never be intimidated into answering questions they did not wish to answer.

'Damn!' the major said shaking his head. 'I know that you're right, but it's a bitter pill to swallow all the same, Hal.'

'And if the sheriff did throw Clu Marvin's dead body in that river, why did he strip him first? That don't make no sense at all, does it?'

The major nodded.

'You're right. Maybe Clu is still alive. But why would his clothing be left on the riverbank?'

'To make us think he's dead,' Cartwright replied.

'Why would anyone want us to think he's dead?' Provine shook his head as he tried to find an answer to his own question.

The deputy licked his lips.

'So that his friends would leave town? If you all thought he'd been swallowed up by that river, you would have to ride on home with your cowboys. Right?'

The major walked around the dry dusty ground absorbing the theory. It was as good a suggestion as any he had been able to come up with himself.

Probably a whole lot better.

'I think that you might be right, Hal,' Seth Provine acknowledged. 'But it still leaves us a whole lot of unanswered questions. Like: why is Brown headed in the exact direction that those outlaws are using to ride towards McCoy?'

'Brown must be in cahoots with Vern Booker and his cronies,' the deputy said. 'It can't be no coincidence that he's on a sure fire route to meet up with the *hombres*.'

Seth Provine gave another massive sigh of frustration.

'Why?' he muttered. 'Why did Brown shanghai young Clu in the Silver Garter? Why is he riding to meet up with men who are wanted dead or alive?'

The deputy rested a hand on the anxious rancher's shoulder and tried to console him.

'None of this makes any sense, Major.'

'But it has to make sense.' Provine

clenched both his fists and somehow managed to keep them at his sides. 'We're missing a vital clue. We must be blind to something that is blatantly obvious to Brown and his cohorts. But what?'

The deputy nodded in agreement.

'Yeah. What has a young cowboy gotta do with Brown and a gang of deadly outlaws? Where's the damn link that ties all this together?'

'Look, Hal!' the major said to the lawman. 'Red and the boys are heading back here.'

Cartwright glanced to his left and looked at the cowboys returning with the rifles and ammunition filling their arms. They had collected their mounts. The well-trained cutting horses ate up the ground as only their breed could.

'C'mon, Major!' he said, heading quickly towards the horses. 'Let's round up all your boys from town and do us some real snooping.'

'What sort of snooping do you mean,

Hal?' asked Provin.

'If Clu is in McCoy, we'll find him. Wherever he is, we'll track him down. If I have to kick down every door in this town, we'll find him and maybe some answers as well.'

'Is that legal, Hal? Are you sure we're allowed to do that?'

'Legal?' Cartwright gave a narrow smile. 'That word has lost a lot of its value in this town since Brown was elected. There ain't a straight official in McCoy nowadays. Nobody that'll give us a warrant or any other kinda legal paper. Nope, we have to find another kinda law if we want to sort out this mess.'

The major knew that the deputy was right.

'Are you sure you want to follow this trail, Hal?'

'Yep. I'm damn sure. We'll start dishin' out some old-fashioned law,' the deputy replied. 'I got me a feelin' that's the only sort Dan Brown's sort understand.'

'What kind of law would that be exactly?'

Cartwright patted the gun strapped to his hip.

'Gun law, Major! Gun law!'

8

The noonday sun was merciless. Even the wide fast-flowing river seemed incapable of cooling the temperature that rose higher with every passing minute. The white-hot desert sand that had already engulfed most of the land east of the cattle town could be seen quite clearly along the jagged horizon behind the four outlaws.

Waves of unseen heat washed over the horsemen reminding them of what they had left in their wake and what they would soon have to return to.

Vern Booker stood in his stirrups, dragged back on his reins and halted his lathered-up mount. Dust drifted across the shallow river towards the black gelding's rider, wearing the gleaming sheriff's star on his leather vest. The outlaw turned and waited as his brother and the two equally deadly horsemen slowed up alongside him.

They were a sight which could have chilled even the stoutest of souls. For each had their own personal arsenal of weaponry and ammunition strapped to their horses. These were professional killers who did not risk their necks by relying on any one favoured weapon. They always had something in reserve. Another gun or another rifle. And the blazing sun danced off the naked metal of each and every one of them.

The cold calculating eyes of the elder Booker narrowed and focused on Dan Brown as he rode straight at them. He knew that there was not one ounce of fear in the dark figure atop the even darker horse.

The black gelding cantered across the river with its master holding the reins in one hand whilst the other rested on one of his trio of gun grips. Even after so many years, he did not trust any of these outlaws. He knew the feeling was mutual.

Booker lowered his rear down on to

his saddle. His whiskered chin touched his bandanna and his eyes watched the familiar figure riding defiantly towards them.

'What you doin', Dan? I thought I told you that we'd meet you at your fancy house. How come you're all the ways out here?' Booker shouted.

'Since when have you bin givin' the orders, Vern?' The sheriff stopped his horse and looked all around them. 'I'm the boss of this gang and don't you ever forget it!'

Vern Booker gave a slight laugh.

'You're gettin' too big for your boots, Dan.'

Brown jabbed his razor-sharp spurs into the sides of his gelding. The startled animal leapt forward and the sheriff grabbed hold of Vern Booker. Both men fell from their mounts and crashed on to the rock-hard ground. Dan Brown hauled the outlaw's head back with his left hand, then sent a powerful clenched fist into the jaw. Vern Booker landed on his back with blood trickling from his mouth. He had forgotten exactly how strong Three Gun Dan Johnson was.

'Ya gonna quit?' Brown snarled.

'OK, Dan. Ya made your point!' Booker said. He spat out blood and got slowly back to his feet. 'You're still the boss of this outfit.'

The three other outlaws dismounted and moved cautiously to the two snorting men. All five stood in a circle. The sheriff spoke first.

'How come ya decided to come to my house and not our secret meeting-place?'

Vern glanced at the other faces before returning his ice-cold attention to Dan Brown.

'We was a tad darned concerned with the telegraph wire ya sent me at Dry Gulch. What are ya thinkin' about, wanting us to go up against the Reno Kid? That's just plain loco.'

Brown grinned.

'Ya dumb fool. It ain't the real Reno Kid I'm wanting ya to tackle. Hell, he'd kill ya all in ten seconds flat.'

Silas Booker pushed his hat back off his tanned features.

'What d'ya mean by that? There's only one Reno Kid, ain't there?'

'Not any longer there ain't, Si.' Brown's grin broadened. 'Me and old Lex Reason have got us another Reno. We found ourselves a young, real stupid cowboy. He's the spittin' image of the Kid and yet he can't even shoot a hogleg.'

The four other outlaws were confused.

'Ya mean a double?' Pern Roberts chipped in.

'Give that man a cigar!' Dan Brown nodded.

'So ya want us to gun down some dude that looks like Reno?' Vern asked.

'Yep! But not in town,' Brown embellished. 'We're gonna send him off towards the desert on a nag that can hardly walk let alone run. Give the young varmint a head start and then go after him. I want him dead before ya brings him back to McCoy. We can't risk him spillin' the beans and tellin' folks who he really is.'

Silas nodded.

'So we'll just look like a bunch of bounty hunters who just got lucky?'

'Yep,' Brown answered.

'Nothin' I likes better than a good bushwhackin', Dan.' Pern Roberts chuckled.

The sheriff inhaled deeply.

'Then you're gonna have one hell of a good time, Pern.'

The four outlaws gathered up the reins.

'Where do ya want us to bushwhack the critter, Dan?' Tom Snape asked as he stepped back in his stirrup and mounted his horse.

Dan Brown gave the dry land behind the four outlaws a seriously long look. He knew it well and also knew that there were few opportunities to ambush anyone between McCoy and Dry Gulch. But there was one spot that fitted the bill perfectly.

'Is that old adobe still near the water-hole, Vern?' the man with the star enquired. 'Ya know the one? About five miles before ya gets to Dry Gulch.'

Vern Booker spat another lump of blood out on to the dry ground, then threw himself on top of his horse.

'Yep. Me and the boys will wait there for the youngster. All you gotta do is make sure that's the way he comes.'

'I'll make sure of that.' Brown grabbed his saddle horn and steadied his horse. 'I'll give him no chance of heading towards the lush range over yonder. He'll have to head for Dry Gulch or into the desert. This kid might be green but he ain't dumb enough to ride into that desert. Even he must realize that there just ain't nothin' out there but sand.'

Vern Booker rubbed his aching jaw thoughtfully.

'When do ya intend letting this kid loose, Dan?'

'Just a little after sundown.'

'Good. That'll give me and the boys

plenty of time to go to the secret hideout, rest our horses up and fix us some hot grub. We'll head on out for the old adobe a couple of hours before it gets dark.'

Dan Brown nodded and watched as the other outlaws mounted their horses.

'Good. Reckon we'll all be a lot richer after this.'

The four outlaws turned their mounts and spurred. They were headed for the well-hidden hideout they used whenever Brown needed their services a few miles up river.

Dan Brown dragged the reins of his black gelding and aimed it back for McCoy. The horse galloped through the shallow river sending ice-cold water spray up over its master.

It felt good.

Real good.

9

A thousand war drums could not have made any more noise than the pounding that exploded inside the cowboy's skull. Clu Marvin had lain motionless for nearly an hour after being violently struck across the neck by the powerful Bruno. The expertly executed blow had paralysed every sinew and nerve in the youthful body. His face was buried in the deep carpet exactly where he had fallen in the centre of the large study. Then, as the drums grew even louder inside his skull, the dazed and confused cowboy felt the delayed pain of consciousness drag him from the blackness of enforced slumber to the reality that he found himself in.

Clu Marvin tried to gather his thoughts together. He lay absolutely still and blinked hard. His only view was from his left eye, which stared across the carpet towards the large, draped study window. A huge dining-table flanked by several chairs reflected the sun off their polished surfaces.

The shafts of golden light caught the dust in the air as Lex Reason and Bruno walked around the room, totally unaware of their hostage's awakening.

Then Marvin heard the unmistakable voice of Lex Reason floating like the dust particles over the expensive furnishings. Its sickly tones reminded the stunned youngster of bitter-sweet molasses leaking from a barrel. He knew that it could consume everything in its path as it spread out like a plague of blackness.

The wooden floorboards beneath the thick carpet moved with every step of the huge bodyguard as Bruno trailed his boss like a faithful yet dangerous hound. Even though they were behind him, Marvin could tell exactly where the lethal pair were in the large room. A fear swept over the cowboy which somehow numbed the pain that emanated from his bruised neck.

The cowboy then began to realize that one of the trio of deadly men who had imprisoned him within the confines of the red-brick house was missing.

Yet although Sheriff Brown was no longer with the other two men, Marvin knew that the danger was still as great. He had already felt the unbelievable power of the bodyguard and knew that men like Reason only existed if they could use a gun. Even though he had not seen any sign of a weapon, the youngster knew that Reason must have one concealed somewhere on him.

The room was hot and a bead of sweat trickled down from his hairline into his eyes. The salt burned like acid but Clu Marvin knew that he dare not move even a muscle. His two remaining captors had to be totally unaware of his having awoken if he were to have a chance of escaping.

Reason walked a few inches away from the cowboy's outstretched hands and carefully stepped over the fingers.

Bruno was less careful and trod on Marvin's right wrist.

Marvin gritted his teeth and refused to allow the pain caused by the heavy bodyguard's boot to enlighten the two men that he was no longer unconscious.

He swallowed hard and watched the men come into his limited field of vision as they strolled towards the window and the twelve-foot-long dining-table.

Reason had not stopped talking since Marvin had woken up but only now could the cowboy's pounding brain actually decipher what the man was actually saying.

Marvin continued to play possum and listened.

'You see, Bruno, this might not be the easiest way to make a considerable profit, but it is certainly one of the best,' Lex Reason said as he rested one of his thin hands on the tall back of one of the many dining-chairs that flanked the table like ranks of soldiers at attention. 'We take one cowboy and clean him up. We then dress him in clothes that reflect the nature of the character we wish him to look like. Then we take him out of town and give him a horse. A very slow horse, of course.'

For the first time Bruno actually managed to find a narrow gap in the flood of words which came from the lips of his employer. He interrupted.

'Ya gonna give him them guns?'

'Of course, Bruno. How could we make anyone believe that our sleeping beauty is the Reno Kid if he isn't armed?'

'Ya gonna give him loaded guns?' the bodyguard asked again with a troubled expression carved into his features. 'He might turn them on us and blow us all away.'

Reason's head flicked back as a muffled laugh escaped his painfully thin body.

'Him shoot at us? Don't be ridiculous. The cowboy hardly knows which end of a gun to hold. I doubt if he could release the safety loops off the hammers without being given instruction. No, my dear Bruno, we have nothing to fear from trash like Clu Marvin.'

The bodyguard was far more cautious than his boss. He had learned a long time ago that it was never wise to underestimate one's enemies.

'I don't know so much, boss. He's young and strong. He might not wanna die just so that ya can collect the reward money on the Reno Kid.'

Marvin felt an ice-cold shiver trace his spine as the words of the bearlike creature filled his mind. It was terror. For the first time since he had been abducted by Sheriff Brown, his worst fears had been confirmed. All the fancy clothes and trimmings were for only one purpose, to make him look even more like the infamous outlaw. He remained perfectly still and tried to work out what he ought to do next.

A thousand confused thoughts raced

through his mind. None of them lingered long enough for him to lasso.

'You worry too much, Bruno,' Reason said as he faced the window and absorbed the rays of the sun with closed eyes. 'I have never once had any trouble getting exactly what I want in this life. I want the reward money on Reno's head and that misfit on the floor will get it for me. That ten thousand dollars is mine.'

'But ya gotta share it with Brown and his gang,' the bodyguard muttered.

Lex Reason turned his head and opened his eyes wide. He stared at the huge creature and then smiled. It was a smile which frightened even Bruno.

'They shall not get a penny of the bounty, Bruno,' Reason vowed. 'Not one single penny.'

'How can ya cut them out? They're the critters who are gonna kill the cowboy and bring back his carcass.'

Reason nodded.

'So what?'

'But ya gotta share it with them or

they'll come after ya, boss,' the huge man said.

Reason placed the palms of his hands together as if in silent prayer and walked closer to the window. The bodyguard trailed the thin figure like a shadow unwilling to release its grip on the object that nature had glued him to.

'Dan Brown has already served his purpose, Bruno,' Reason explained in a hushed tone. 'I think that it is time that I capitalized on my investment with him also.'

'Huh?' The large man leaned down and looked hard into the skeletal features. 'What ya mean?'

'I spent a thousand dollars getting Brown elected. He has already managed to bend the law enough for me to have seen a few of my plans make a healthy profit, but now is the time for me to exercise my power over him and his followers.'

'Ya gotta talk American, boss.'

'Brown and his gang in Dry Gulch are worth roughly five thousand dollars collectively, Bruno.' Lex Reason's eyes sparkled in the bright morning sunlight. 'Once they have killed the cowboy and Brown gets authorization to collect the ten thousand dollars reward money, I shall let it be known that he is none other than the notorious Three Gun Dan Johnson. I shall be forced to tell Deputy Cartwright that Vern and Silas Booker and their associates are in Dry Gulch.'

Bruno looked concerned.

'Ya gonna get them all killed for the bounty?'

Reason patted the cheek of his bodyguard.

'Well done, Bruno. I knew it was only a matter of time before you would understand.'

'This is darned dangerous, boss.' Bruno sweated. 'Them boys will turn on ya for sure.'

'I'm not scared of them. Are you?'

'Yep! Real scared.'

Clu Marvin licked his dry lips. He had heard every word that had spilled from the thin-lipped Reason. The cowboy realized that he had to act quickly if he wanted to live. Yet he knew that the doors of this mansion were well secured.

If he were to attempt escaping, Clu would have to be sure that he could get out into the open air before the bone-crushing hands of the bodyguard got hold of him.

That would require him to find a turn of speed which the two men could not match. But would his legs obey him after he had lain helplessly on the floor for so long? The question taunted the young man.

His heart began to pound faster as the laughter of the thin man near the window echoed around the wood-panelled study. It was like the sound of a coyote baying at a night sky.

Marvin knew that it was now or never.

There might not be another chance.

The two men were facing away from him.

The cowboy pushed himself up off the carpet, raised his knees until his bare feet were planted firmly. He crouched low, trying to use the table and chairs for cover. With both men looking out of the window at the panoramic view of the cattle town, Clu made his move. Silently the cowboy raced across the room, scooped the boots up off the floor and then pulled them on to his naked feet.

Marvin's eyes were fixed on the cardboard box that still rested on the edge of the table. He knew that the guns and belt inside might just help him keep the two deadly men at bay. He slowly raised himself up to his full height and edged towards the cardboard box and the handsome set of six-shooters which rested inside.

Then the words of Lex Reason rang out in his mind.

The deadly dangerous man had been correct. Marvin barely knew how to use a gun, but was also well aware that he had to learn. And learn damn fast.

In one swift movement the cowboy reached into the box, hauled the gunbelt out and swung it around his narrow hips. Marvin buckled the belt clumsily, when suddenly he saw both men turn their heads and look straight at him.

Clu Marvin's jaw dropped. So did those of the two men.

Then Reason shook and yelled at the top of his voice as his bony right hand reached for the .38 secreted under his left arm in a hand-tooled holster.

'Quickly. Get him, Bruno! Get him!'

10

Like the bear he so resembled, Bruno raised both his arms and growled. His huge fingers and thumbs clawed at the air as the bodyguard tried to obey his boss's orders. The terrified Clu Marvin was grateful that the solid wooden table was between him and the snarling man who had started to move far faster than the cowboy would have thought possible.

Then Clu saw the sunlight dance across the silver barrel of the small pistol in Lex Reason's bony hand. It was aimed straight at him.

'Stand still, sonny!' the thin man commanded.

The cowboy was more fearful of the bodyguard's huge hands than he was of Reason's bullets. There was no way he would obey such a command and risk being torn apart.

Not wanting to suffer Bruno's fury for a second time, the terrified youngster kicked one of the chairs at the big man's legs, then turned on the heels of the new boots and ran for his life into the hall with the vaulted ceiling.

The highly polished marble floor did not lend itself to having brand-new boots race across its mirrorlike surface. Clu felt himself lose his balance; he went head over heels. He slid and crashed heavily into the front door. He was winded for a few endless seconds. Clu Marvin knew that he was still in trouble as the rants of his pursuers bounced off the sturdy walls. The cowboy quickly dragged himself up and started to attack the door's bolts and handles. His hands fevishly tried everything to open it.

It was impossible.

Then he heard the heavy boots behind him. They were close. Too close. Marvin looked over his shoulder and saw Bruno standing with his powerful arms outstretched.

The man was grinning. It did not suit him.

'Ya need a key to open that door, sonny! Ya needs keys to open all the doors in this place. And I got the keys in my pants' pocket. Ya wanna try and get 'em?'

The terrified cowboy spun around and squared up to Bruno. He tried to swallow but his throat was like a desert. He could see the shape of the large keys against Bruno's right thigh beneath the blue trousercloth.

A man could be ripped apart trying to obtain those keys, he thought.

'I reckon I'll leave them be, Bruno,' Clu Marvin replied. His eyes narrowed as he watched the huge bodyguard slowly close in on him.

There was death in his dark eyes.

'Ya don't want to kill me, Bruno!' Clu said.

'Sure I do!'

'But think about it, what'll ya gain by murderin' me?'

Bruno's smile widened.

'I'll enjoy myself, sonny!'

Desperately, Clu Marvin looked all around the hall. He then returned his attention to the beast before him. No grizzly bear could have filled the cowboy with more trepidation than the bodyguard did.

He had to do something fast!

But what?

Then Marvin remembered the guns that hung on his hips. His fingers scratched at the safety loops until they came off the gun hammers. He dragged both weapons out of the holsters and aimed them straight at Bruno.

'Stop or I'll shoot ya, Bruno!'

Bruno did stop but then started to roar with laughter. It echoed all around the hall until the cowboy felt as if the entire building was mocking him.

'Back away!' Clu shouted. 'Back away or I'll have to shoot ya!'

Bruno was unafraid.

'Pull them triggers, sonny! Go on. Pull them!'

Clu Marvin inhaled until his chest

felt as if it would explode and then squeezed the triggers. To his surprise, nothing happened. He could not hide his confusion.

'Why don't they fire?'

Bruno laughed even louder and once more started to move towards the confused cowboy.

'Ya dumb little egg-sucker. Don't ya know that ya gotta cock the hammers first? Them's real guns, not the kinda homemade trash cowpunchers use.'

The cowboy was still no wiser.

Then the large man leapt. It seemed an impossibility that anything quite so obviously heavy could throw itself across open space, but that was exactly what Bruno did.

The cowboy had faced a few loco mavericks in his time riding for Seth Provine over the years, but none of them could hold a candle to Bruno.

A startled Marvin hesitated as he watched the huge man flying at him. He felt the large hands catch both his shoulders and send him violently backwards. The sheer force lifted the cowboy off his feet. Both men crashed heavily into the solid door and slid to the floor. Somehow Clu managed to free himself and scrambled from beneath his attacker.

With the guns still in his hands, Marvin raced across the vast expanse of marble floor towards the corridor which he recognized as leading to the rear entrance of the building.

Suddenly a blinding flash of hot lead cut through the air ahead of the cowboy and hit the wall. A chunk of wood panelling was torn off a corner. A cloud of splinters showered over Clu and stopped him in his tracks. It was quickly followed by the deafening sound of Reason's pistol being fired and echoing all around the hall.

A burning sensation ran down Marvin's left arm.

He had been winged.

His elegant shirt-sleeve was covered in the red gore that had erupted from the flesh wound. Marvin turned and looked into the large study. He saw Lex Reason standing with the smoking gun in his outstretched hand.

The cowboy went to move again, when he saw the barrel of the gun spew out another cloud of smoke. Another deafening sound tortured his brain. He felt the heat of the bullet as it passed within inches of his face.

Frantically he tried to cock the hammers of the guns in his hands. It was a skill that he still could not grasp or master.

'Bruno!' Reason yelled out as he started to move towards the terrified cowboy. 'I've winged him, Bruno. Finish him off!'

Clu's eyes darted back to the front door.

The huge man had risen from the floor. He snorted and charged like a bull seeking the flesh of a matador to sink its deadly horns into.

Marvin knew that he had to think fast. Faster than he had ever done before.

It was now a matter of survival!

One mistake would be his last.

A fraction of a second before Bruno's colossal bulk reached him, Clu leapt to his right and watched the bodyguard miss him and fall heavily. The huge bear-like creature slid across the gleaming marble floor and disappeared into the dark corridor.

'Marvin!' Lex Reason shouted out.

The youngster hesitated and saw Reason still heading at him with his pistol aimed in his direction.

'Stand still and you'll live!'

'Not for long by the sounds of it!' Marvin replied, holstering both the weapons he still had not worked out how to use. He moved one way and then the other and prayed that Reason's next bullet would not get as close as the first one had. He saw a brass hatstand out of the corner of his eye and kicked it at the thin figure.

Reason side-stepped the hatstand and squeezed the trigger of his gun again. Another bullet blasted through the air and narrowly missed its target. A tall highly decorated vase beside the cowboy shattered into countless fragments.

Clu Marvin crouched and quickly looked to his left and then right.

There was no escape via either the front or rear doors of the large house. Then he looked at the magnificent staircase and its expensive carpet, which led back up to the landing.

Perhaps there might be a way out up there, his fevered brain screamed out inside his throbbing skull.

Another bullet blasted at Marvin.

He twisted and turned before bolting up the thick carpeted staircase two steps at a time. Two more bullets flew over his head. Plaster from the high ceiling showered over the cowboy like snow as he reached the landing.

Again he ducked.

The cowboy tried to catch his breath. He heard the grunting below his high vantage point. Marvin gritted his teeth and watched as the bloodied Bruno rushed from out of the shadows past his boss and started up the staircase after him.

Now the big man's features were covered in blood that poured from deep gashes on the top of his head. The unblinking eyes were fixed on the cowboy.

No man with blood coursing through his veins could have been anything but totally afraid of the gruesome sight.

Clu's heart pounded even faster as once again terror overwhelmed him. He rose back up and raced down the corridor which he knew led to the room he had bathed in earlier. A room which had a window that led to a porch roof.

He slammed the door behind him.

His hands searched for a key in the lock. To his horror, there was no key.

Marvin looked around the room as he heard the heavy footsteps of his pursuer echo in the corridor. Then he saw the ornate chair next to the bed. He grabbed out and dragged it to the door. He rammed its wooden back to brace it under the brass doorknob.

He knew he had bought himself a little time, but how much time would depend on how quickly Bruno could smash his way through the wooden door.

A minute?

Perhaps only seconds.

I gotta get out of here fast! he told himself as the door began to buckle under the battering Bruno's shoulder was inflicting upon it. Shafts of splintered wood cracked in the panels. Then Marvin saw the furious blood-stained face of the bodyguard peering at him through the holes.

'I ain't gonna wait for Dan Brown to finish ya off. I'm gonna kill ya myself, cowboy!' Bruno roared as his shoulder kept on hitting the door. The frame came off the wall as the chair slipped from beneath the doorknob.

Marvin backed away.

The tall window beckoned.

The cowboy grabbed a sheet off the bed and held it before his face. He ran for all he was worth and threw himself at the six-paned window. Marvin felt it give as the sound of shattering glass and breaking wood cascaded all around him.

He fell ten feet before being stopped abruptly. He was on the shingled porch roof. Marvin rolled over and freed himself from the sheet. Slivers of razor-sharp glass dropped off him as he got back to his feet. Then he heard the door cave in above him. Bruno had entered the bedroom.

Somehow the cowboy managed to stagger and then run the full length of the porch until he heard the screaming voice behind him. Only when Marvin had reached the end of the porch did he look back at Bruno's head poking out of the window.

He looked at the ground below. It was an awful long way down but the cowboy jumped anyway.

Marvin landed in the rear garden, rolled over and landed on his feet. He recognized the wooden fence with the loose board straight ahead of him.

This was the way that the sheriff had brought him the previous night, he thought.

He scrambled over the slippery ground to the sun-bleached fence. His fingernails pulled at the boards until he found the one that was hanging by a single nail. The cowboy forced the loose board aside and tried to get through the narrow gap. At first he could not seem to manoeuvre his lean body. Then Clu realized that the twin-holstered gunbelt had made him at least four inches wider than when he had last slipped through its tight gap.

'I'm still comin', cowboy!' Bruno's voice rang out as the large man dropped from the window on to the porch.

Marvin turned sideways and forced himself between the wooden boards into the alleyway.

Then he heard the sound of something far heavier than himself landing in the rear garden. The grunts made it clear that Bruno was still on his tail. Like a savage beast, the giant had the scent of his prey in his nostrils.

Before Clu Marvin had a chance to move a muscle, the entire wall of wood crashed down on top of him. Its weathered boards disintegrated as the massive bodyguard charged into it.

The cowboy was violently knocked off his feet by what was left of the planks. He lay on his back blinking hard as if trying to rid his eyes of the sawdust which temporarily blinded him.

Then he focused up at the snorting Bruno who stood over him.

'Reckon I'm gonna save them boys a lotta trouble by killin' ya all on my lonesome, sonny!'

Before the cowboy could say anything, the large hands reached down and grabbed at Clu's throat. The thick fingers encircled his entire neck, squeezing with unbelievable fury. The youngster could not call out or even breathe. It felt as if his eyes were going to explode from their sockets.

Bruno lifted him off the ground by his neck and started to shake him as if he were nothing more than a rag-doll.

'Ain't so damn smart now, is ya?'

Marvin could feel his life coming to an end. He used the last ember of his strength to haul one of the guns from its holster, then he struck out blindly. One blow followed another as the barrel of the Colt kept hitting the already blood-covered head.

Then the cowboy heard the sound of his attacker's skull cracking.

The deadly grip around his throat loosened. Bruno fell like a tree and landed on top of him. Even as he choked for air to pass through his crushed windpipe and fill his lungs, Marvin was still able to hear Lex Reason's chilling voice.

He summoned another burst of strength and pushed at the dead weight that had him pinned to the ground. It did not want to be moved.

The cowboy listened to Reason's voice grow louder as it vainly called out to the bodyguard. At last Clu managed to slide from under the motionless creature and get back to his feet. He holstered the bloody weapon and steadied himself.

'Bruno! Answer me, Bruno!'

Clutching his throat with a shaking hand, Clu looked up and saw the thin man by an open window. The cocked gun in the skeletal grip was aimed straight at him.

As the wounded Marvin staggered along the alleyway, he heard the gun fire once again behind him.

The cowboy's lean frame was almost knocked off its feet by the powerful impact which caught him in his left shoulder-blade.

He continued to stagger away from the red-brick house even though he knew that the bullet had found its target.

11

The haunting sound of Lex Reason's venomous gunfire refused to quit and continued to echo all around the lone rider as he drove his mount up from the well-hidden ravine into the outskirts of McCoy. Sheriff Dan Brown pulled back on his reins and stopped the black gelding abruptly. He stared ahead up the dusty trail which twisted its way between the large maple trees and scattered houses which flanked the opulent red-brick mansion owned by the wealthy businessman whom even he feared.

His fear was not based on anything physical, for he knew that he was far stronger than the thin man. He was also well aware that he was far better with any of his three guns than Reason. Even the massive body-guard did not trouble him in the slightest degree, for he knew that even the largest of creatures did not have hearts strong enough to withstand a well placed bullet. His fear was based on the knowledge of the strange businessman's past deeds. For Lex Reason had a reputation for not being a man you could afford to trust. He would destroy anything if there was a profit in it. Brown knew that there would come a time when he was no longer a valuable asset to the man who lived in the large red-brick house.

Brown steadied his eager horse. There was an air of disbelief in the hardened horseman. He could see curious souls peering out of doors and windows, vainly trying to set eyes upon the unknown gunman who had violated their precious space. They too wondered where the shot had come from. For this was a part of McCoy which never suffered the brutality that the rest of the cattle town was plagued by. This was where the rich lived in their splendid homes. Every single one of them had been built from the profits their owners had accumulated off the backs of the men and women who worked near the railhead.

The filthy reality of the town near the hundreds of stockpens, filled with prime cattle ready to make their last journey to the eager Easterners, never touched the streets filled with maple trees.

These were people who paid their taxes to shield themselves and their families from anything distasteful, anything that even hinted of the deadliness that festered in the rest of McCoy.

The aroma of penned steers at the railhead over a mile away which could not be controlled, the lawyers, judges and businessmen paid well for protection that could keep such unpleasantness at bay. To hear a shot in their neighbourhood was unthinkable.

Yet Dan Brown, just like the stunned people who looked out from their windows and doors, could still hear the echoes of the shot swirling in the midday air.

He, unlike them, knew that there was only one place that it could have come from. Yet Brown was confused. What was going on? When he had ridden down to meet Vern Booker and the rest of his gang, the cowboy was unconscious.

A chill traced its way up his backbone.

Could the cowboy have managed to escape? If so, there was a possibility that he would tell someone of what had happened to him. How he and Reason had tried to make him look like the Reno Kid simply so they could kill him and claim the fortune on the outlaw's head. Even though Dan Brown wore the sheriff's star, he knew that would not stop his enemies from gunning for him.

And he had more enemies than most.

Enemies who would enjoy turning their weapons in his direction and squeezing the triggers.

He heeled the black gelding beneath him to turn full circle as his hooded eyes studied the scene all around him. Apart from the curious faces, there was no hint that anything untoward had happened in or around the well-kept area.

Brown gripped his reins tightly and steadied the skittish mount.

His brain tried to work out who could have fired the shot that had awoken an entire section of McCoy. But there were really only two men who could have done so. The question was: was it Lex Reason or was it perhaps the cowboy?

Either way, he knew he had to find out fast.

The sheriff had gathered up his reins and leaned forward over the saddle horn when the sound of another shot rang out. This time Sheriff Dan Brown was absolutely certain that it had come from the direction of Lex Reason's red-brick home and the barrel of the wealthy businessman's .38.

The sound of the small-calibre weapon was in total contrast to the expensive Colt .45s that Reason had purchased for the cowboy to wear.

The lawman turned the horse, spurred hard and drove the black gelding along the dusty trail which led to Reason's mansion.

With every stride of the horse's long legs, Dan Brown felt that he was getting closer to his own ultimate destiny. What that destiny might be was something he refused even to dwell upon. All he knew for sure was that it would have the familiar fragrance of gunsmoke.

12

The cattle-pens that flanked both sides of the rail tracks seemed to go on for ever. More than half were filled with the prime Texan white-faced steers brought to McCoy by Major Seth Provine and his seasoned team of cowboys and wranglers. There was a constant noise of troubled cattle bemoaning their fate, which was only rivalled by the sound of millions of flies. The blazing sun only seemed to make matters worse as the great locomotive slowly rolled along the gleaming steel rails into the very heart of the busy town, with its string of fifty stock-cars trailing between the boiler and the caboose. Black smoke and sparks billowed from the tall chimney-stack and rolled over the stockpens as cowpokes started to assemble with their long prodding poles gripped firmly in gloved hands. Soon they would start to force the white-faced steers up the loading ramps into the stock-cars.

Major Seth Provine stood on the high auctioneer's platform looking at the activity below him as his trail scout Able Jones led the cowboys he and ramrod Red White had rounded up towards the line of wooden buildings.

The straight-backed man nodded proudly to himself as his wrinkled eyes focused down on the cowboys coming from the distant livery stables astride their well-trained mounts. He saw Hal Cartwright riding beside Toke Carter, holding the reins to his own dappled grey stallion.

Red White slowed his horse and watched the major descend from the high platform and come towards them. He had never seen the rancher's face look quite so grim.

It troubled the seasoned cowboy.

If the major was worried, there had to be good reason for all of them to be the same.

'Did any of you boys hear gunshots a few minutes ago?' the retired officer asked as he took his reins from Toke and mounted his tall horse.

The cowboys had heard nothing above the sound of the locomotive and cattle. Neither had Hal Cartwright.

'Probably thunder, Major,' the deputy said. 'I never heard nothin'. These steers kinda drown out every-thin'.'

Provine was not convinced. There was not a single cloud in the big blue sky above them.

'I've heard a lot of weapons being fired in my time, Hal. I've also heard a lot of thunder. I definitely heard shots.'

'Comin' from where, Major?' White asked as he steadied his cutting horse.

'I'm not sure, Red. This town is so big and spread out, it could have come from any direction. It was gunfire though. I'd stake my life on that.'

'How many shots?' Carter asked.

'I only heard the two.' The major sighed.

'Weren't no shoot-out then.' Jones nodded knowingly. 'Not unless one of the critters managed to nail his man damn quick.'

'Two shots about two minutes apart,' Provine added.

Cartwright eased his horse to the side of the grey.

'Ain't no reason for ya to get troubled, Major. I doubt if it had anythin' to do with young Clu. More than likely it was a drunk fool lettin' off a little steam. Ya hears that kinda ruckus most nights of the week around here. Bet ya that's all it was.'

Provine's eyes darted at the deputy.

'I wouldn't take that bet, son. A man could lose his grub stake betting on something as thin as that.'

Toke Carter turned his horse and looked at the major.

'What we gonna do, sir?'

'We're going to ride through every street and alleyway until we find Clu, Toke,' Provine answered.

'What if we don't find him?'

'Then I start kickin' down doors, boy,' Hal Cartwright was interrupted. 'I'll find your pal.'

'Any particular doors?' Able enquired.

'Reckon I got me a couple in mind to start with.' the deputy spat at the ground. 'But we gotta check out every one of McCoy's streets first. Check out any ditches deep enough for a body to be lying in as well.'

'Body?' Toke gulped. 'Does that mean ya reckon that Clu's dead, Deputy?'

Seth Provine could see the distress in the cowboy's face. He was a man only a year or so older than Marvin. He raised a hand and waved it at Carter.

'Steady, Toke. You have to be strong. Hal here only means that some thief might have hurt Clu for his trail pay. He might have hogtied him and left him in a ditch or even under a porch. We have to check every single place that's big enough for a full-grown man to be hidden.'

'He might be dead though, huh?'

Toke Carter pressed.

Provine slowly nodded.

'Yes. He might be.'

Deputy Cartwright eased his mount alongside the troubled Provine. He patted the back of thc older rider.

'If it's OK with you, I figure that we ought to start our search in the main street, Major.'

'That's agreeable, Hal.' Provine nodded.

Toke Carter steadied his buckskin quarter horse.

'I just had me an idea, Major. Why don't I go and get Clu's horse from the livery?'

'Why, son?' Provine asked.

Toke leaned across to the major.

'I heard tell that horses are like hound dogs. They can find their masters in the dark. Ya reckon that's right?'

Provine shrugged. He had no idea whether the youngster was right or wrong but could not see any reason why he should not allow the distressed cowboy to at least try.

'Go on, Toke. Get Clu's horse. Let's see if the critter can find him. We'll start in the main street like Hal says. You can join us when you're ready.'

'OK!' Carter stood in his stirrups, dragged the head of his horse around and spurred. Dust flew up off the hoofs of the galloping quarter horse as its master headed back to the livery.

'Ya reckon the young 'un could be right, Major?' Cartwright asked. 'Can a horse sniff out its master like he thinks?'

Major Seth Provine teased his reins and started his mount walking. The rest of the riders kept pace with the grey.

'No I don't. But I'm praying real hard that he proves me wrong, Hal.'

The trail scout Able Jones chewed on his tobacco and looked across at Provine.

'There was talk amongst some of the boys that they was teasin' Clu that he looked like the picture of the Reno Kid on the Wanted poster pinned outside the sheriff's office, Major.'

'Able's right, Major. Toke and a few of the boys did tease the youngster about him lookin' like the outlaw,' Red White added. 'They said that the sheriff overheard them.'

'Really?' Provine frowned before turning to Cartwright. 'Is that right, Hal? Does Clu actually look like this Reno Kid character?'

'I ain't real sure,' Cartwright replied. 'I've not looked at any of the posters close up. Dan Brown pinned up the posters a week or so back.'

'I seen it, Major,' White said. 'The Reno Kid looks just like young Clu. Never seen anyone look so much like one of them pictures before.'

'Any objection if I take a look at that poster myself, Hal?' the major asked the deputy. 'I've a feeling that it might have something to do with Clu going missing.'

Cartwright rubbed his chin.

'I ain't got no problem with ya takin' a look, Major. I reckon we all ought to go look at it. I'm a mite curious about it myself now.'

'C'mon then!' Provine raised himself off the saddle and used his experienced hands to urge the stallion on.

The rest of the riders spurred to catch up with the powerful grey stallion.

13

There was a trail of blood leading along the dry alleyway to where the wounded cowboy rested in between two well-cultivated bushes. The shade of a tall maple kept the blistering sun off the injured youngster's back, a back that still bled from the small bullet hole in the left shoulder-blade. Clu Marvin had carried the bullet in his back for more than a quarter of a mile before he had fallen on to his knees at the rear of another of the large houses. He knew that he needed a fast horse to carry him away from this nightmare. Yet so far he had not set eyes on anything with more than two legs.

The cowboy was hurt.

Badly hurt.

The shirt which only thirty minutes earlier had been in pristine condition was now torn and soaked in blood. But

Clu Marvin cared nothing for the condition of his clothing, all he could do was try and think of how he might survive this ordeal and have a chance of living long enough to see another sunrise.

Yet trying to string even a few rational thoughts together was proving more difficult as he lost more and more precious blood. His entire body was racked with torturous pain. It was something which he had never experienced before and for that small mercy he was truly grateful. This was something a man only wanted to feel once in his lifetime, or not at all.

The wound throbbed mercilessly. It felt as though a red-hot branding-iron had been pushed into his shoulder-blade. Only the bone had stopped the lead ball travelling right through his lean body and out of his chest.

He rubbed his face and tried to think.

Marvin had managed to put enough distance between himself and the lethal gun barrel of the strange Lex Reason; he knew that he was no longer in range or sight of the vicious man. But he was still in trouble.

Big trouble.

Suddenly something caught his attention and managed to alert his dulled senses. It was the sound of pounding hoofs ringing out all around his resting place. The cowboy dragged himself up and stared hard down the narrow back road. It was a trail which wound its way, like a sidewinder, around the expensive properties and their acreages.

Someone was coming, he told himself.

A rider. It might be the sheriff returning. If it was Brown astride his horse, Clu knew that he had somehow to get that horse. But how could he take on someone like Dan Brown? Even uninjured he was no match for the likes of the sheriff.

A cloud of dizziness filled his head. He clung to the branches all around him and waited for the terrifying feeling to pass. He fell back on to the hard ground again.

As Clu regained his thoughts, he tried to understand how he of all people had fallen into the mess that had enveloped him. It was no use. He could never fathom the devious minds of those like Reason or Brown.

All he was still certain about was that there was no one to help him find sanctuary in this unfamiliar place.

The sound of the horse's hoofs grew louder.

The rider was getting closer.

With no help of any kind, Clu had to somehow get out of McCoy. He had to flee this unholy town whilst there was still life in him.

Somehow ride away from this place of pain.

There just had to be a safe haven out there somewhere, didn't there? He seemed incapable of convincing himself of that simple fact.

Every instinct told him that he had to escape before one of his enemies finally finished the job they had started. He knew that Lex Reason was still alive and so was Dan Brown. For all Marvin knew, the burly Bruno might also have survived having his skull cracked open.

How could he get away from them?

Sweat dripped like rain from his face as he forced himself back up on to his feet. He rested his full weight against the trunk of the tree beside him.

He thought about Major Provine and the rest of the cowboys he had not seen since the previous day. He knew that the major always gathered up his crew and set out for home at exactly nine in the morning the day after he had sold his herd. The sun was high above him. It had to be at least noon, he judged. Provine and his friends must have left McCoy and set out for Texas hours earlier. He had no idea how much his fellow Texans thought about him.

Marvin rubbed the sweat off his face with his sleeve and tried to think. How could he get help?

The sheriff was part of the ruthless

gang that wanted to kill him for the reward on Reno's head. So if he could not go to the law for assistance, who else was left?

Who could he trust?

No matter how hard Clu tried to think of an answer, he failed. He was alone and for the first time in ten years, he had no one to help him.

He drew one of the Colts from its holster and looked at it with ignorant eyes. The six-shooter gleamed in his blood-covered hand but it did not help him. He tried to pull back its hammer with his thumb but did not realize the hammer had to click three times before it locked fully into position. Clu was too weak and too confused to learn new tricks. He shook his head and slid the .45 back into its handsome leather resting-place.

The sound of the hoofs caught his attention once more.

His eyes were glazed as he staggered toward a small porch and rested his arms on its whitewashed handrail.

Then he saw a coiled rope hanging on a nail at the side of the house beside him. He might not be any good with the guns which hung on his hips in the holsters, but he knew how to handle a rope.

Even half-dead, he was still a cowboy.

He might not be the brightest star in the universe, but he was a damn good cowboy. And good cowboys knew how to use ropes the way townsfolk knew how to cut flowers.

Marvin staggered a few steps and dragged the rope off the wall. He then returned to the porch with the coil of rope in his hands. Instinctively he uncoiled the the rope until the bulk was in his left hand whilst his right made a wide lasso loop.

The sound of the approaching horse grew even louder and drew him to the bushes once more.

Clu used the dark green bushes and tree trunk as cover. His eyes narrowed and focused on the rider who was galloping along the back trail towards him. A cloud of dust floated and hung on the hot air behind the rider. Marvin remained perfectly still and watched his target like a hawk studying its prey.

Only his hands and fingers moved as they continually toyed with the rope. Then the cowboy recognized the rider.

'Brown!' he said angrily.

For a brief moment, the cowboy felt a savage fury inside him that he had never experienced before. Maybe it was the fact that he hurt so badly. Whatever it was, for the first time in his life he knew what it felt like to want to kill another man.

For a few beats of his pounding heart, he actually wanted to destroy the sheriff.

Somehow Clu managed to ignore his dark thoughts and calm himself down. His right hand started to move in circles and cause the loop of the cutting rope to twirl beside him and then above his head.

A thousand hornets could not have equalled the sound that came off the fast-moving rope.

Marvin continued to keep the rope swinging in ever greater circles over his head as he watched the unsuspecting horseman thunder past his hiding-place back to Lex Reason's home.

'Now ya gonna taste rope, Sheriff!' Clu Marvin whispered in a low snarl.

With a flourish of skill and power which defied the agony that racked his body, Clu stepped out from his hiding-place, took aim at the rider atop the black gelding and released the large looped rope into the air.

The cowboy watched as it floated in a perfect circle above and over the head of the sheriff before he jerked back on the rope slack. The perfectly aimed lasso fell over Dan Brown's shoulders. Clu had done this countless times with steers but never once used his skill on a man before.

Marvin's right hand gripped at the length of rope and tugged it back with all his might.

The startled sheriff felt it tighten

around his middle and then he was being dragged backwards off his saddle. He rolled over the gelding's tail and crashed on to the stone-hard ground.

The sound echoed around the back trail.

Clu Marvin somehow managed to run at the fallen lawman. With each step he recoiled the rope to ensure that there was no slack left when he reached the winded Brown.

With a speed of hand that belied his injuries, Clu Marvin tightened the rope and wrapped it around the hands and feet of the stunned sheriff.

A dazed Dan Brown opened his eyes as the cowboy secured the last knot and moved to the gelding.

'What ya doin' to me?' the sheriff protested as the cowboy caught hold of the horse's bridle.

Marvin held the saddle horn, stepped into the stirrup and slowly hauled himself on to the black gelding. He swung the horse's head around and stared down on the helpless man.

'If I only had me a branding-iron, I'd use it,' the cowboy said honestly.

Suddenly a shot cut through the sunshine. It came close. Too close for comfort. The spooked gelding reared up and forced Clu Marvin to hold on for dear life until its forelegs landed on the dusty ground once again. The cowboy looked over his shoulder and saw Lex Reason less than fifty feet behind him, waving the smoking pistol in his hand. His index finger pulled vainly on the trigger as the hammer's firing-pin fell on spent shells.

'Even I know when a gun is empty!' Marvin called out.

Reason screamed and ran towards him and the hogtied Brown.

'You're a dead man, sonny!'

'C'mon, hoss! Get goin'!' The wounded cowboy whipped the horse's shoulders with the lengths of his reins, then kicked hard with the heels of his boots. The black mount leapt over the helpless lawman and galloped down the trail.

Reason reached Brown, knelt and untied him. The sheriff got to his feet.

'A horse! I need a horse!' Brown shouted. 'I gotta catch that varmint and break his damn neck!'

Lex Reason pointed to the home of one of his neighbours a few yards from where they were standing. It had a well-constructed stable in its back yard.

'Judge Thomas has a fine palomino in that stable, Brown. Go get the damn thing and catch that cowboy before he gets away. He's worth ten thousand dollars to us.'

The sheriff ran to the whitewashed stable and opened the unlocked double doors.

'Will he mind if I borrow his horse?'

Reason shook the spent shells from his gun and searched his well-tailored jacket pockets for fresh bullets.

'Just take the horse. Judge Thomas will not complain.' Reason snorted. 'You could say I own that horse.'

Dan Brown led the palomino out into the bright sunlight. He threw a blanket over its wide back and patted it down with a gloved hand.

'How come?' the sheriff asked as he lifted the horse's saddle off the ground and threw it on top of the blanket. 'How can ya own his horse? I don't get your drift.'

'Well, I already own the judge.' Reason sneered with a twisted smile etched into his thin features. 'And if I own the man himself then I must own the horse as well. Correct?'

The sheriff shrugged.

'Ya lost me there.'

'Hurry up.' Reason sighed heavily. 'He'll be back in Texas by the time you start after him.'

Dan Brown hastily secured the cinch straps under the belly of the handsome horse, dropped the fender down and stepped into the stirrup. The man with the star pinned to his vest mounted and then swung the palomino away from the stable.

'He won't get far!'

Reason nodded.

'Bring him back dead!'

Brown spurred feverishly and drove the magnificent horse into the trail dust that still hung on the dry air.

Before Lex Reason had finished reloading his weapon, the rider had disappeared from sight. The thin man slid the hot weapon in the shoulder holster beneath his left arm and headed back towards the large red-brick house.

All he could now was wait.

14

The four outlaws had made good use of the time that they thought they had before setting off for the old adobe water-hole. They had taken the heavy saddles off the backs of their exhausted mounts and allowed them to drink their fill of the cold river that passed within yards of their secret hideout a mile or so from the outskirts of McCoy. They had also made a fire and were enjoying a meal of bacon, biscuits and coffee when they heard the sound of the galloping mount.

'Who in tarnation is that?' Silas Booker asked. He was polishing the long barrel of his Springfield rifle with his bandanna as he sat next to the fire.

His brother rose and walked across the dry ground towards the river and their mounts. He pulled a screen of bushes aside and screwed up his eyes to get a better look at the rider.

'It's Dan ridin' like the devil is on his tail,' Vern Booker said. Then he corrected himself. 'Hold on there, that ain't Dan but I'd bet a new hat that's his horse though. Come look.'

The other three outlaws rushed to Booker's side and stared out into the heat haze.

'You're right!' Pern Roberts sniffed. 'That's Dan's horse but it ain't Dan on it.'

'Who'd be loco enough to steal Dan's horse?' Tom Snape queried. 'There ain't no such animal. That has to be Dan.'

'Ya blind bat!' Vern removed his battered Stetson and slapped the outlaw hard with its brim. 'I say's it ain't Dan in that saddle. That's some other *hombre*.'

'But who?' Silas continued polishing his rifle.

'Whoever it is, he ain't too smart,' Roberts noted drily. He returned to the fire and his half-full cup of black coffee.

'What ya mean, Pern?' Vern asked as he returned his hat to his head. 'Ya mean by stealin' Dan's horse? That is kinda crazy.'

Roberts sat down and picked up his cup. He blew into it before taking another sip.

'That ain't what I means.'

'Then what?'

'Is ya all as dumb as that rider? Can't ya see where the fool is headed?'

The three men all returned their attention to the trail of dust that cut its way through the swirling heat haze.

'Damn!' Vern Booker gasped. 'The critter is headed straight into the desert!'

'You're right!' Silas shook his head in amazement. 'That rider is gallopin' to a place where there ain't nothin' but sand.'

'Sand and an awful lotta sun,' Vern added.

Roberts nodded.

'That's what I was tryin' to tell ya. He's either real green or real stupid.

Or both maybe.'

'He'll be buzzard bait for sure.' Snape shrugged.

Vern Booker laughed.

'It ain't our problem. Let's have some more vittles.'

Tom Snape cupped the palm of his hand to his ear.

'Ya hear that?'

'Hear what?' Silas asked.

'There's another horse comin' this way, boys! And he's comin' damn fast.'

Vern Booker drew one of his guns and cocked its hammer until the weapon fully locked.

'Whoever he is, he'd better not come anywhere near here or I'll kill him for sure,' he growled.

15

The raging rider atop the galloping palomino had spurred and whipped the mount mercilessly in his desperate desire to catch and kill Clu Marvin. Dan Brown had known that the cowboy was already five minutes ahead of him and that meant he was already out of the range of his trio of deadly six-shooters. He cut down through the narrow lanes and crossed the wide street before forcing the horse to descend through the brush he knew would cut down the distance between himself and his wounded prey.

Brown had lashed the animal beneath him with the ends of his reins until blood could be seen on both the golden shoulders of the palomino. But the sheriff had not given a damn at the punishment he had inflicted and was still inflicting on the mount. All he could think of was getting his hands on the cowboy.

The tall horse had leapt across a fallen tree and then drove on down towards the shallow river and the dried-up land beyond. The lawman knew that the cowboy had headed for the river blindly as most strangers to this part of McCoy always did. For there was no hint of the dead land which lay only a few miles across the cool river.

Every now and then, Brown had caught sight of hoof-tracks on the soft soil as he forged on and on. The rider hauled back on his reins just enough to slow his mount without actually stopping it. He grinned as he saw the churned-up ground left by his own black gelding as Clu Marvin had driven it down towards the well-hidden ravine.

'C'mon!' Brown had shouted as he sank his spurs back into the wide-eyed mount and cracked the reins across the animal's tail. The golden horse had blindly galloped on.

As he had ridden down into the shadows of the well-nourished trees which only grew on his side of the river, the sheriff knew that the cowboy could not maintain the distance between them for long. Clu Marvin had stolen his horse to make his escape and the black gelding was already lathered-up and in need of grain and water. The horse beneath him had a turn of speed he had never experienced in his own horse.

It was only a matter of time before he reduced the distance between them and the cowboy was in range of his guns. Brown doubted that even a fit youngster could not take more than one bullet in his wide back.

Even though the tracks left by Marvin's mount were still easy to follow, Brown dragged his reins to his left and forced the palomino to take a different course. His secret hideout was less than a mile away beyond the wall of brush and he knew that his gang would still be there.

He aimed the palomino and again spurred.

The palomino had ridden up from the ravine and out into the blazing sun. The soft, muddy ground along the riverbank had barely slowed its pace as Dan Brown forced the tall animal towards the hidden campsite used by his gang. The horse's long legs had splashed up river, the animal had only slowed its pace when its master dragged back on the reins as his cold eyes saw the four outlaws with their weapons aimed straight at him.

'It's me, ya fools!' Brown shouted out at them.

Vern Booker lowered his gun and exhaled heavily. He could not conceal his disappointment.

'Damn it all! It's just Dan,' he groaned.

The sheriff dropped from his saddle and led the palomino to the men who looked disappointed that they had not been able to fire their arsenal of weapons at him.

'What the hell was ya aiming ya guns at me for?' Dan Brown asked the sheepish outlaws as they once again gathered around the fire.

Vern crouched down and picked up his tin mug. He then filled it with the last of the coffee from the blackened pot and stared into the steam.

'I reckon ya lost ya horse, huh?' He grinned.

Brown glanced around at the faces of the other men. They were all smiling.

'Quit smilin' and get them damned horses saddled up fast!' he ordered. 'That horse-thief is the same critter you're meant to be bushwhackin' later.'

'What?' Roberts asked. 'Ya mean he escaped? How?'

'Just do as you're told!' Dan Brown snarled, his hands resting on his gun grips.

Vern Booker finished his coffee, rose to his feet then kicked soil over the fire until only blue smoke remained.

'Ya heard him, boys. Saddle up.'

The lawman stared over the shallow

river as the men started to prepare their horses for riding.

'Which way did he go?'

'The loco bean headed towards the desert, Dan,' Tom Snape said, shaking his head.

'Are ya sure?'

Snape nodded.

'Yep!'

Silas Booker rubbed his chin.

'Why would the kid ride into the desert, Dan?'

'Maybe he was confused by the bullet in his back.' Brown spat and wiped his mouth on his sleeve. 'And it ain't exactly obvious that the desert is over in that direction if'n you're a stranger in these parts.'

Booker nodded.

'Who put a bullet in his back?'

'Lex!' Dan Brown responded with a wry smile etching his features.

'Should have figured that.' Vern shrugged. 'His sort always prefers shootin' folks who are facin' away from 'em.'

'We gotta get that cowboy, boys,' Brown insisted.

The four outlaws gave a united groan.

'Ya think we're as loco as him?' Silas asked as he slid his rifle into its scabbard. 'Nobody rides into that desert if'n they got a brain in their heads.'

'We have to catch and kill the critter and take him back to town,' Brown said. 'That's the only way we can claim the reward money.'

Tom Snape tightened the cinch straps of his saddle.

'Ya want that bounty? Then go get it, Dan. It's plumb loco riding into that desert. It's deadly. I ain't goin' and ya can't make me.'

Dan Brown's eyes narrowed. He released his grip on the reins and turned on Snape. He marched across the damp ground towards the outlaw beside his mount. Snape turned and went to raise his fists when the lightning-fast blow caught him squarely on his jaw. He grabbed at the shoulders of the stronger man, then felt the knee catch him in his belly.

Snape gasped and dropped like a stone at the feet of the ferocious man.

'You're ridin' into the desert with me. OK?' Dan Brown shouted at the outlaw.

Snape nursed his jaw and spat blood on to the mud between his legs. His eyes darted to the other outlaws before returning to Brown. He looked up at the angry outlaw and then reluctantly nodded.

'OK,' he managed to gasp.

'Anyone else got any objections to followin' me out into that desert?' Brown snarled as he looked at the three outlaws in turn. ''Coz I'm hankerin' to kill me someone and that don't just mean that cowboy.'

They stared at him. All they could see was the clenched gloved fists of the man who had ruled them with sheer strength and brutality for longer than any of them cared to recall.

Vern Booker ran a hand down the neck of his refreshed horse and then stepped into his stirrup. He mounted the animal and gathered in his reins.

'We'll ride with ya Dan.'

'Damn right ya will!' Brown said.

The five men had canteens filled with the ice-cold water from the fast-flowing river. They would require every single drop of it.

16

Ahead of the lone horseman there was nothing as far as the eye could see except a cloudless blue sky and an ocean of white sand dunes. They rolled in all directions making it impossible for the cowboy to have even the slightest clue to his whereabouts. He was lost. If anything living had ever crossed the virgin snow-coloured granules before, there was no evidence of it.

The cowboy doubted that even Satan would have willingly ventured into this place of death.

He dragged the reins to his chest and felt the throbbing pain in his back again as the horse stopped. He tried to blink and rid his eyes of the burning salt that encrusted his lashes and lids but even that hurt.

Clu Marvin knew that he had to find somewhere to rest before the sun fried what was left of him. Somewhere there had to be a safe haven in this wilderness of sand, he thought. There just had to be. Yet where?

He could no longer even rely on his honed cowboy skills to guide him. For everything looked exactly the same. Each dune was the same as the last. Smooth and with no distinguishing marks. He was used to a land of brush and the odd tree to tell him that he was at least travelling in the right direction. The occasional distant mountain also helped him to steer a true course across most unknown lands.

But here, there was just sand.

Apart from the hoof-tracks behind his mount, there was nothing to tell his confused mind which direction he had come from to reach this blisteringly hot place. He looked over his shoulder and watched as even the hoof-tracks started to disappear as dry sand hurriedly filled the depressions left by the gelding.

For all he knew, he might be riding in circles. He might have already been to this spot before and the desert had covered his trail to fool him.

Briefly Marvin glanced at the sky again. The sun was now lower and yet no less intense. Darkness could not come fast enough. He stared at his burned hands. The skin was a cruel shade of red from the relentless rays.

There was nowhere to hide.

Yet Marvin knew that he could do nothing except continue riding onward, for there was no returning from this devilish place. Not whilst the deadly riders continued to trail him.

They were manhunters.

He ran his fingers through his bedraggled sweat-soaked hair and wondered how long he could keep going. He lifted the canteen off his saddle horn and shook it. The sound of one last mouthful echoed inside it.

The cowboy knew that he would have to ignore his own thirst and let the tired horse have that last drop of the precious liquid.

His fevered mind had tried to work

out how there were so many horsemen following him. It failed. He had counted five of them the last time he had found a high enough dune to look back from, but the shimmering heat haze played tricks with his tired eyes.

Were there really five riders on his trail? Or just one determined killer whose image danced in the sickening waves of heat? There was no way of knowing for sure. Nothing made any sense to the cowboy any longer.

Everything was confused.

Clu Marvin had never even heard of mirages in his brief and, until now, uneventful life. He thought the dancing images might be a sign that he was losing his mind.

But the cowboy had no idea that the heat haze had already saved his bacon more than once since the five horsemen had been on his trail. It had made his own image dance and shimmer enough for the usually deadly accuracy of Silas Booker to miss with his trusty long range Springfield single-shot rifle.

Clu gasped for air and tried to think.

Could thirst make a man go insane?

Was he already loco?

His mind was filled with so many thoughts and yet few made any sense to him. The cowboy was ill-equipped for this dangerous desert, as were most men who ventured into its unforgiving reaches. He had not even realized that there was such a place so close to the famed cattle town. Yet, even if Marvin had known that his desperate flight would bring him here, he knew that he would not have had time to fill the half-empty canteen that hung next to the sheriff's unused saddle rope.

Clu had fled from killers in human form. Men who doggedly still remained on his trail. And yet he had found himself in the grip of another sort of killer. One that consumed everything that dared to challenge its insatiable hunger.

The desert of death was like a living entity. It grew and moved silently. Its dunes rolled ever onward and burned all that they touched and enveloped.

Were the five outlaws more deadly than the sun and sand?

This mysterious desert could kill the healthiest of men quickly. Even the cowboy realized that those with an untended bullet wound like his had virtually no chance of survival.

For more than four hours the rider had forced the black gelding on and on in a vain attempt to outrun his pursuers. Yet they had continued to follow. Marvin was certain that it had to be Dan Brown and the gang he had talked to Lex Reason about in the large red house, on his tail.

Men like Brown would not quit, as less blood-thirsty creatures might. They wanted to slaughter him and get the reward money too badly to give up so easily.

They knew that Marvin was no match for them. Even without a bullet in him, he was like a new-born calf amid a pack of hungry wolves.

Clu Marvin had seen little of what

had at first only faced him and now encircled his exhausted mount in every direction. A pain which had been even more intense than a hundred red-hot pokers had kept his eyes shut tight as his head hung over the neck of the galloping horse.

He had not even noticed the sand until it was too late. Until there was nothing else left to see but sand. The blisteringly hot sun seemed to have no mercy or limitations to its deadly intensity.

It continued to get hotter with every passing second.

Wherever Clu Marvin looked it was the same terrifying landscape. Was there sanctuary over the next dune? he asked himself.

Perhaps there was an oasis with clean fresh water just another mile or so ahead of him. He had to try and convince himself that there was something out there in the ocean of sandy waves. Something that might save him.

Yet Clu Marvin was getting weaker

with every passing heartbeat. He knew that the bleeding had stopped but the pain seemed to grow worse.

Again he forced the black horse up to the top of another high dune so that he could look back. The gelding was as tired as the man who sat in its saddle. The horse slowly obeyed and reached the flat of the dune and then stopped as Marvin eased back on the reins.

The cowboy raised a hand and shielded his eyes against the low sun. For a moment he seemed to see nothing but a blur of moving air. Then his eyes focused on the black outlines of five riders and their mounts. Brown and his gang seemed to float above the sand in the heat haze.

'They're still comin', boy.' Clu sighed heavily. 'They ain't ever gonna quit. I'm buzzard meat for sure.'

The horse snorted as if in agreement.

Then a flashing light amid the five riders caught his attention. Clu rubbed his eyes with his sunburned hands and focused at the horsemen. The sun danced off the long barrel of Silas Booker's rifle.

Once again, the outlaw had pulled the Springfield from its saddle scabbard to try and hit his chosen target.

Before the cowboy could do anything he felt the horse beneath him buckle from the powerful impact before giving out the most horrific cry he had ever heard. Then the sound of the rifle fire caught up with its bullet and filled Marvin's ears.

It was too late.

The black gelding fell to its side with its stunned rider still in the saddle. Clu hung on to the reins for dear life as he and the animal rolled over. For a heart-stopping moment, the cowboy thought he was going to be crushed. Only the softness of the sand prevented the full weight of the gelding doing just that. Then the heavy creature slid down the white sand and took the wounded rider with it. It did not stop until it reached the foot of the dune.

Clu Marvin dragged himself clear of the dead horse and stared at the wide red trail of blood that covered the white wall of sand.

He got to his feet and looked down in disbelief. The bullet had passed through the saddle latigo and main cinch and then straight into the body of the horse. Marvin hovered above the animal's body and watched as gallons of blood pumped out of the wound and soaked into the sand at his feet.

It was the most sickening sight he had ever seen.

'By the looks of it, that varmint got ya plumb centre in the ticker, boy,' the cowboy said as he plucked the canteen up off the saddle horn and draped it over his injured shoulder.

Clu winced and then instinctively ducked as the sound of another rifle bullet passing high above the top of the dune echoed all around him.

For some unknown reason he then picked up the coiled saddle rope as well and hooked it over the gun grip which poked out from the holster on his left hip.

Even more dead than alive, the thirsty youngster knew he had to use the valleys between the dunes if he were to continue his nightmarish quest for sanctuary.

Clu Marvin started to walk slowly as the heat continued to beat down on him. With every staggered step he took, he found himself praying for two things.

The first was for water and the second was simply for the sun to set.

17

With the deafening noise of the still-smoking single-shot Springfield rifle resounding in the five riders' ears, Silas Booker rocked in his stirrups and yelled out triumphantly at the top of his voice.

'I got him! Did ya see, boys? I got the varmint! Shot him clean off his hoss!'

Dan Brown shook his head and looked sideways past Roberts, Snape and Vern at the rejoicing outlaw as he waved his rifle above his head and balanced in his stirrups.

'Ya shot my black gelding, ya swine!' he growled.

The younger of the Booker brothers sat down and looked at the faces of his four companions.

'You're wrong, Dan. I shot the cowboy.'

'Nope. Ya shot my horse!' Brown repeated.

'Are ya sure?' Silas scratched his bearded chin.

'I can't be certain but it sure looked like ya hit the horse to me, Si,' Vern Booker said quietly out of the side of his mouth.

Silas Booker thrust the rifle back into its scabbard beneath his saddle and sighed heavily.

'I'm plumb sure I hit the cowboy, Vern. Honest.'

'Ya killed my horse.' Brown snorted angrily. 'I paid a hundred dollars for that animal.'

Tom Snape's head turned to Brown.

'Ya actually paid for the horse? Ya losin' your grip, Dan?'

'Sure I paid for it. Hell, I'm the sheriff. I can't go stealin' a horse, can I?' Brown spat at the ground and wiped his mouth along his sleeve.

Snape shrugged.

'Shame. Shame to pay that much for somethin' and then have Silas shoot it.'

'Shut up!' Silas shouted. 'I still say I hit the boy.'

'Ya keep believin' that, Si.' Vern patted his brother on the back. 'There ain't no harm in it.'

Dan Brown gathered his reins in his hands and looked around the strange scenery. The dunes were starting to worry, secretly, even him. There were two of the huge obstacles between themselves and where they had last seen Marvin.

'We ain't gonna find out who is right or wrong until we ride over to that damn hunk of sand. C'mon!'

The four outlaws watched as Brown spurred the palomino and rode in the tracks of their prey straight up the first massive dune.

'It'll be dark soon, Vern,' Tom Snape whispered. 'That darn sun is real low.'

'I know.' Vern Booker nodded. 'Least ways it'll be a tad cooler.'

'I don't cotton to being out here after sundown,' Snape added. 'How we gonna follow that cowboy's trail in the dark?'

'Beats me,' Booker said honestly. 'Maybe old Dan'll figure that out.'

'Mark my words, boys, he'll be the death of us all,' Pern Roberts sighed.

'C'mon, ya worthless pack of vermin!' Dan Brown shouted out behind him as he drove the palomino on across the white sand.

'Reckon he wants us to follow,' Vern Booker said. He tapped his spurs into the sides of his mount and encouraged it on after the determined Brown.

They followed.

18

The large moon had taken over sentry duty from the sun above the desert of sand just as the cold had replaced the heat. Clu Marvin had no idea where he was heading or of anything else for that matter. All his fevered mind knew for sure was that the shadows offered him a shield of protection that the merciless sun had not. He had tried to increase his pace, knowing the five horsemen now had the advantage. They still had their horses and he was on foot.

They should be gaining on him and he knew it. Yet he was so tired. More tired than he had ever been before.

So far the cowboy had managed to keep away from those who sought his life. The large bright moon cast a million black shadows off the shoulders of the dunes and he instinctively used every one that he encountered. For even good trackers could not easily find footprints in the darkness.

Marvin had walked aimlessly in the desert for more than two hours since his horse had been shot out from under him. The sun had set less than thirty minutes after he had headed out on foot from the bloody carcass, yet time now meant nothing to him. The empty canteen swung back and forth on his shoulder. It kept pace with each of his stumbling steps. He wondered if he would ever be able to fill it again with the precious liquid that in a place such as this was worth more than gold.

The odds were not good.

A million stars sparkled like precious gems and taunted those below the night sky as they had done for an eternity. But the cowboy had neither the strength nor the ability to look up any longer. Marvin's head drooped as if it had increased in weight, whilst his sunburned chin rested on his chest. His glazed eyes stared at the sand as his feet somehow managed to take one painful step after another.

Simply being alive was now torturous.

The eerie blue moonlight spread itself over the dunes in total contrast to the black shadows.

'Water,' he mumbled and continually repeated through swollen lips.

He was now too weak to even lift his feet off the sand as he walked. His right boot slid forward, as it had done countless times before, when something hard beneath the sand prevented the simple action. Clu Marvin lost his balance, stumbled and then tripped. He had no strength left in his tortured body to stop himself from falling.

The cowboy landed on his face like a rag-doll.

For what seemed a lifetime he just lay there. He mustered every ounce of what remained of his courage and forced himself back up on to his knees. A blinding pain surged through him. He then felt blood trace a route down his side from the bullet hole in his back.

'Gotta keep goin'!' he told himself as his hands searched in the shadows for the rope and the empty canteen. Yet it was not the familiar objects that his fingers located in the sand, but something solid.

The very thing which had tripped him.

It was a curious Marvin who moved on all fours towards the hidden object just behind his boot-heel. His hands located it again and brushed the sand away until the remnants of a small wall were revealed to his blistered eyes.

'A wall?' he gasped in total surprise as he questioned his own sanity. 'I've found a damn wall out here in the middle of a desert?'

The sound of two gun hammers being cocked behind him made the cowboy slowly turn on his knees and stare into the strange blue light. Then he saw the guns and the man holding them at hip-height emerge from the blackness.

'Yep. You found a wall in the middle

of the desert!' the voice confirmed.

Clu sighed and felt defeat overwhelm his pounding heart. His eyes tried to focus on the face of the gunman but it was impossible.

'Ya might as well shoot me now,' the cowboy said. 'I knew it was only a matter of time before ya caught up with me.'

The gunman advanced.

'What the hell are you blabbering about, stranger? I ain't been trailing you.'

Marvin tilted his head back and smiled.

'I reckon ya gotta be one of Dan Brown's men. So shoot. The way I feel, it'd be a mercy. I'm just about done for anyways.'

'Who are you?' the man asked as he trained both barrels at the cowboy. 'And who is Dan Brown?'

Clu Marvin could see the face of the man more clearly now that he was closer. It looked familiar but his dulled mind could not recall where he had seen it before.

'We ever crossed trails before?'

'Nope!' the gunman said. 'I'd have remembered you.'

The cowboy rubbed his face and screwed up his eyes.

'Ya sure looks familiar.'

'That's a mighty fancy shooting-rig you got there,' the man said. 'Only a gunfighter would wear something that expensive on his hips. Are you a gunfighter?'

'Nope. I'm just a cowboy. And Dan Brown's a sheriff, but he's kinda crooked. He got himself a gang and they've been trying to kill me.'

The man holstered his left gun whilst keeping his right aimed straight at the youngster. He then cautiously knelt beside the cowboy. His free hand inspected the blood-soaked creature before him.

'Looks like they already done half the job.'

Marvin gave a pitiful laugh.

'Yep. They've nearly done for me

and no mistake.'

'Why would they try to kill you if you're just a cowboy though?' the man asked as he helped Clu Marvin back up on to his feet. 'That don't make no sense at all. Not even for a crooked sheriff.'

'They reckon I looks like some outlaw named Reno,' Clu croaked. 'They figured on killin' me and claimin' the bounty on this outlaw. They fixed me up with clothes and these guns.'

'Reno?' the gunman slid his other gun into its holster and started to lead the cowboy into the shadows. 'You mean the Reno Kid?'

'Yep. That's his name,' Clu Marvin confirmed as he felt the man taking his weight and guiding him deeper into the shadows. 'The Reno Kid. Ya ever heard of him?'

The gunman cleared his throat.

'Yep. I heard of him OK, stranger.'

'I never heard of him myself. Not until me and my trail-drive pals seen his Wanted poster back in McCoy.'

Marvin's face was twisted by pain again. 'Ya say that you have heard of him?'

The man nodded.

'Yep. In fact I reckon it's only fair of me to tell you that I am the Reno Kid.'

'Ya are?'

'Yep. I am.'

Even with a mind filled with fevered confusion, the wounded cowboy had enough wits about him to wonder where the gunman was taking him.

And why?

All he could see ahead of them was blackness.

Total blackness.

19

If the young cowboy had not been so weary he might have realized that the small wall he had stumbled over was part of something far larger that the desert sand had engulfed countless years earlier. If his mind had not been starved of precious water for so long and his battered and bleeding body drained of so much blood, he might have been able to understand where the Reno Kid was taking him.

The notorious outlaw had recognized the resemblance between the badly injured Clu Marvin and himself. Athough he was quite a few years the cowboy's senior, Reno knew that the image on the Wanted posters was taken from an old photographic likeness of him. The only one he had ever had taken back when he was still young enough not to realize that it might fall into the hands of the authorities. It showed him when he too was in his earlier twenties.

Marvin was now only able to walk with the assistance of the Kid's helping hand.

'Where we goin', Reno?' the cowboy kept asking.

Reno had not replied. He simply helped the younger man over the soft sand down into a deep gully beside a towering dune until they reached a place that only the outlaw knew existed. An elegant horse stood where it had been left with its saddle still on its high back.

'I smell a horse somewhere around here, Reno,' the cowboy muttered.

'You must be a cowboy,' the Kid noted. 'Only a cowboy could smell a horse without being able to see it.'

'Where we goin'?' Clu asked again.

Eventually, Reno answered the cowboy's simple question.

'Open your eyes, stranger. We're here.'

Clu Marvin leaned on the stronger man and blinked hard until his top and bottom eyelids separated. A shaft of moonlight glanced across the almost hidden edifice before them. At first the cowboy was confused and for the umpteenth time did not trust his eyes. They had betrayed him too many times since he had been hit by Lex Reason's bullet. He lowered his head and shook it in a vain attempt to clear his mind.

Clu then looked up and sighed. He was still filled with disbelief.

The archway of sand-coloured bricks was intact. Whatever lay above was like everything else in this ferocious land, completely covered by the dunes. But beyond the archway there was some sort of dark room. A single candle-flame flickered inside on an ancient table.

'What is this place?' Clu asked.

'An old wine cellar,' Reno replied. 'This used to be some kind of monastery or suchlike. That was before the desert came and swallowed up all the land. I figured the cellar was below ground level and that's why it's still intact.'

'How old is this place?' Marvin limped weakly forwards with the support of the Kid until they entered the cool interior of the cellar.

'Who knows? The Spanish probably built it. It could be a couple of hundred years old I guess,' Reno said, easing the cowboy on to a hardback chair next to the table. 'I guess there must have been a lot of grapes growing around here at one time.'

'How do ya figure that?' Clu asked. He rested an arm on the edge of the table and looked up at the man who had helped him.

Reno pointed to a corner of the brick-built cellar.

'Well, look. What do you see?'

Marvin stared at the well-constructed wooden racks. There must have been a 1,000 or more bottles resting on specially made shelving. He had never seen anything quite so neat before.

'Is that wine?'

Reno nodded and strode to the rack, pulled off a bottle and returned to the injured cowboy. He placed the bottle next to the young man and turned the label toward him.

'Read that,' the Kid said.

'I can't read,' Marvin admitted.

'It don't matter none,' Reno said. He picked up a corkscrew and expertly removed the cork from the neck of the dusty bottle. 'It ain't in American anyways.'

'How did ya find this place?' the cowboy asked.

Reno shrugged.

'A few years back I had me a posse dogging my tail. I had a full canteen of water and led them into this desert. I reckoned on circling the critters and then heading down to Dry Gulch. I found this place by accident.'

'What happened to the posse?' Clu enquired.

Reno smiled and did not answer.

'Ya got any water, Reno?' Clu asked

as his head rolled on his thin neck. 'I ain't tasted none in an awful long time.'

The Kid walked to the opposite end of the cellar. The cowboy's eyes trailed the man trustingly. He then saw the water-pump and bucket.

'You want water? I got me a whole well of the stuff.' Reno smiled as he lifted the bucket and returned to the table and rested it down beside the wine-bottle. He shook a tin mug, scooped out a full measure and handed it to the youngster. 'You drink as much as you can hold. Wash those eyes of yours as well.'

Both men's attention was drawn to the horse outside the archway as it started to snort nervously and drag its right hoof across the sand.

'What's spooked your horse?'

Reno quickly checked both his guns.

'Something sure has. I'll take me a look outside and see if them five back-shooting *hombres* are anywhere close.'

Clu downed the cool liquid and then

filled the mug again.

'Ya be careful, Reno. Them critters are bad.'

Reno smiled and removed his jacket.

'Correction, stranger. I'm bad. I'm the Reno Kid. They just think that they are. If they get too close, I'll have to teach them the difference.'

Before the cowboy could say another word, the infamous outlaw had silently disappeared out into the mixture of moonlight and shadows. Clu drank the water and then washed the dust and salt from his eyes. He then refilled the tin mug again.

He had no idea what was about to happen. Even someone without a bullet in his back would never have guessed what would happen in the next thirty or so minutes.

But the cowboy was certain it would have the acrid aroma of gunsmoke.

20

The eyes of the five outlaws darted suspiciously all around them as they eased their mounts to a halt amid the sea of sand. They stared down at the abandoned canteen and coiled rope bathed in moonlight. Dan Brown dismounted with a gun in one hand, crouched down and plucked the empty canteen up and moved toward Vern Booker.

'This is my canteen, Vern,' said the outlaw with the sheriff's star pinned to his vest.

'He's gotta be darn close now, Dan!' Booker nodded. 'More dead than alive by my reckoning. I can smell that reward money already.'

'He must be out of his mind to leave the canteen.' Brown smiled in agreement. 'Only a critter loco from loss of blood and lack of water leaves his canteen when he might find himself something to fill it with.'

Silas Booker eased his horse next to Brown as the man hung the canteen on the saddle horn of the palomino.

'Look at them tracks, Dan.' Silas pointed at the churned up sand. 'Look!'

Brown glanced down.

'What? It looks like the ground's all messed up 'coz the cowboy fell down. So damn what?'

Silas dropped from his saddle, moved across the soft ground and knelt down. His eyes studied every mark etched into the soft surface.

'There were two men here, Dan. Two, not one.'

Brown's expression altered. The smile evaporated and was replaced by a concerned frown.

'That ain't possible! The cowboy is on his own. Ya all know that. Ya seen him. He's alone!'

Roberts and Snape joined Silas Booker on the sand and also studied the ground carefully. They too saw the two sets of footprints leading away toward the dark shadows.

'He's right!' Tom Snape said. 'There were two critters who walked away from here.'

'Two men walked off over yonder, Dan,' Pern Roberts added as he aimed his trigger finger.

'If there are two sets of tracks,' Brown paused for a moment as he felt a cold shiver trace his spine, 'then who is the other critter? And where in tarnation did he come from?'

'I don't like this!' Snape said. 'Could be some dude that likes to bushwhack folks.'

'We ought to wait for sunrise!' Silas suggested.

'Yep. Wait until we can see what we're facing,' Snape drawled. 'I don't cotton to them shadows none. Not when there's someone out there.'

Vern Booker eased himself off the horse and walked to where Roberts had pointed. He screwed his eyes up and stared into the dark shadows as his hands drew both guns from their holsters. He cocked their hammers and glanced at Dan Brown.

'They can't have gone far. We gonna go find 'em?'

Dan Brown nodded.

'Yep. Vern's right, ya yella vermin. Reckon we better go and finish that cowboy off. We ain't gonna get that reward money unless we can produce a body.'

Silas dragged his rifle from its saddle scabbard and walked away from the five horses to the four other outlaws. He slid a bullet into the chamber and then bit his lip.

'I don't like this, Vern,' he admitted.

'What don't ya like, Si?' Vern asked.

Silas was nervous.

'Who do ya reckon that other dude is? What's he doin' out here in this desert? Who is he, Vern?'

Dan Brown walked toward the shadows, pulled two of his trio of guns from their holsters and cocked their hammers. He knew it was dangerous, but he wanted that money so bad he could taste it.

'I'll tell ya who that critter with Clu Marvin is, Si! He's the dude that'll end up just as dead as the cowboy is gonna be when I gets him in my sights.'

'I sure hope so.'

Vern inhaled deeply.

'Let's mosey, boys!'

The five outlaws spread themselves wide and walked, with their arsenal of weaponry primed, into the black shadows.

Suddenly a flash of deafening gunfire cut through the darkness. A red taper of hot lead carved a route through the evening air and hit Tom Snape dead centre. The impact knocked the outlaw off his feet.

The four stunned outlaws dropped to their knees and frantically fired back in the direction that the shot had come from as Dan Brown checked Snape. The deadly accurate bullet had gone straight through the stricken outlaw's heart.

‘How is he?’ Vern Booker shouted out above the sound of their gunfire.

Brown spat at the sand.

‘Dead!’

21

With the agility of a desert fox, the Reno Kid ran up the unstable dune and threw himself across the crest of the sand. He had only used a single bullet and yet he had already killed one of the men who were hunting the cowboy.

Reno had not waited for Dan Brown or any of his gang to even see him. He had picked off Tom Snape and then moved to higher ground.

There was a good reason for this.

For Reno knew that these outlaws were back-shooters. To him they were not worthy of any consideration. They had trailed the young cowboy and driven him as close to destruction as was humanly possible. They had plucked a simple cowboy off the streets of McCoy so they could kill him.

The irony of it all was that they wanted the cowboy to be mistaken for him. They wanted to claim the reward on his head, but did not want to face the real Reno Kid. He was angry about that.

Dan Brown, Pern Roberts and the Bookers were also angry. They were angry because someone in the shadows of the dunes had not only the skill, but the defiance to take them on. They had thought they were faced by a half-dead cowboy who had no knowledge of the guns they had supplied him with.

Now the helpless man was being championed by another.

Someone who not only knew how to use his guns, but also knew how to kill.

They advanced through the darkness. This time they kept low, not wanting to be the next victim of their unseen enemy's lethal accuracy.

But the Kid, unlike them, was used to this place. It was like a second home to him. It had afforded him protection from all those who had wanted to claim his reward money. He had spent a lot of time here hiding from the law over the years.

Reno ran across the rim of a dune, then dropped on to his belly and rested on the ridge of soft, cool sand. He watched the four cautious creatures below as they proceeded through the valley of sand.

The high dune offered his keen eyes a perfect view of everything below him.

Dan Brown led Roberts and the Booker brother deeper into the unknown. Moonlight glinted off the barrels of their guns and rifle.

The Reno Kid squinted hard down at the men below him. There was something familiar about two of the outlaws. His crystal-clear memory instantly recognized the two Booker boys. Silas by the Springfield rifle he was never seen without and Vern by the way he held his guns so far away from his body.

The Reno Kid had seen them a few years earlier, trying and failing to rob a bank in a small Arizona town. A town with a sheriff so old and deaf that even a cannon being fired next to him would have not awoken the pathetic soul. Yet the Bookers had managed to get it all wrong. He had remained in the window of a saloon playing five-card stud during the entire exercise in incompetence.

'Is that you, Vern?' the Kid called out from his high vantage point.

The four outlaws stopped in their tracks and waved their guns around, trying to figure out where the voice had come from.

Brown knelt down and looked across the shadowy sand at both the startled Bookers.

'Who the hell was that, Vern?' he called out.

'I dunno!' Vern Booker swallowed hard and tried to pinpoint where the voice had come from above them. It was a waste of time for the Kid had already moved across the high wall of sand.

'Is that Silas with you?' Reno called out again.

Silas moved to the side of his brother and clutched at his rifle desperately.

'Who was that, Vern? How come he knows us?'

'There!' Dan Brown shouted.

The three outlaws turned and watched as Brown jumped away from the wall of sand and aimed both his guns up at the top of the nearest dune. He fired both guns blindly.

Vern Booker edged forward to the side of the man with the sheriff's star pinned to his vest.

'Did ya get him, Dan?'

Brown was about to reply when two shots rang out from above them. Two deadly shots.

Vern Booker twisted on his heels and fell heavily beside the stunned outlaw leader. A bullet had hit him in the nape of his broad neck. Brown raised his guns to return fire when he saw Silas Booker stumble toward him.

The bearded man dropped his

beloved rifle and then started to shake. He fell across the body of his brother.

Brown stared hard into the expressionless face.

'Are ya hit, Si?' Brown asked before noticing the damp patch on the outlaw's shirt. Then he saw the small bullet hole.

Pern Roberts ran from the bodies and knelt, clutching his smoking Colts in shaking hands.

'Let's get out of here, Dan!' Roberts screamed. 'Whoever that is up there, he's pickin' us off darn easy. Ya comin'?'

Brown shook his head.

'I ain't goin' no place until I kill me somcone.'

'Fine!' Roberts got back to his feet and ran for his life past the bodies and Brown. He did not stop running until he was back at the five horses. The terrified man holstered both his guns and then pulled his mount away from the others. He grabbed the saddle horn and stepped into the stirrup. He threw his right leg over the wide back of the horse and landed on the saddle.

Roberts gathered up the reins and then heard a voice to his right.

'You going somewhere?' the Kid asked.

The outlaw glanced over his shoulder and saw Reno stepping out of the shadows. His hands were hovering above his holstered gun grips.

Roberts' right hand went for his gun and almost managed to pull it from its holster when he saw Reno draw and fire in one fluid movement.

The horseman felt his neck move as the bullet went cleanly through his throat and out of the base of his skull. For a split second Roberts sat in his saddle totally unaware that he had been killed. Then he rolled to his right off the saddle.

The skittish horse bolted, taking its master with it as his boot remained rammed in the stirrup. The lifeless body bounced on the sand as the galloping horse disappeared into the desert, dragging it in its wake.

Reno ran back into the shadows and climbed up the closest dune until he had reached the highest point he could find. He stared down at the figure below him as Brown continued to edge his way deeper along the gully.

The Kid realized that Brown was getting too close to the secret cellar and the badly wounded cowboy. He had to stop him before he finished the youngster off.

He fired down into the shadows and saw the figure stagger until he was no longer in view.

Reno moved quickly over the soft sand and descended as fast as he could. The sand was dry and gave beneath him.

Suddenly Reno felt himself sliding out of control. He lay back and plummeted feet first down the dune. Faster and faster he felt his body moving until his shirt began to rip from the friction.

Then his boots hit the top of the brick archway above the cellar entrance and he stopped abruptly. Reno felt as though every sinew in his body had been ripped from the bones. He shook for a few moments, then saw Dan Brown a few yards away on the floor of the sandy gully.

Brown raised both his guns and fired.

The bullets missed and Reno leapt down. His boots hit the sand. He rolled over and drew a Colt from its holster. Reno squeezed the trigger and watched as one of Brown's guns was torn from his left hand.

Dan Brown shook his hand and then saw that the bullet had also severed his small finger.

'Ya low down sidewinder!' Brown yelled out as he raised the gun in his right hand. 'Ya shot one of my fingers off. Now you're gonna pay for that!'

Reno went to shoot when he heard the hammer of the Remington New Model Army .44 fall on a spent shell. Dan Brown's jaw dropped.

'Now ya got me!' Brown snorted as he threw the weapon at the Kid.

'I'm not a man to take advantage,' the Kid said. He holstered his gun and brushed the sand off his sleeves. 'I'll let you pick up that Army .44 and reload it. Then we draw.'

Brown continued to shake his bleeding left hand.

'Who are ya?' he asked.

The Kid turned and started to walk towards his horse.

'They call me Reno. Are you Dan Brown?'

'That's what they call me nowadays, Reno,' the sheriff said as his right hand snaked to his third holstered weapon. He gripped the Starr Double Action Army .44 and cocked its hammer as quietly as he could. 'You might know me better as Three Gun Dan Johnson.'

The Reno Kid heard the name and realized his error. He had thought the man was unarmed. He spun on his heels and drew both his guns.

It was too late.

The Starr fired.

The Reno Kid felt the power of the

bullet. It punched him hard in his chest and lifted him off his feet. He landed heavily on his back. He felt both his guns flying from his hands a fraction of a second before the back of his head hit the compacted sand.

Three Gun Dan Johnson ran to the stunned unarmed Kid and stared down at the face.

'Damn, ya do look like that cowboy.'

'You're wrong, Johnson. He looks like me,' Reno corrected as he stared into the barrel of the .44 and heard it being cocked again.

Suddenly there was a deafening sound. It was like thunder. It made the man with the gun in his hand spin on his heels before he fell dead beside Reno.

The dazed Kid pushed himself up on to an elbow and looked at the archway to the cellar. The cowboy stood there with the smoking Colt in his shaking hand.

'I finally figured out how to use this darn thing, Reno,' Clu said.

'You did good, cowboy.' Reno smiled. 'Real good.'

Clu Marvin slid the gun into its holster and then saw the infamous outlaw close his eyes and fall back on the sand. He staggered to the outlaw and knelt down beside him. He pressed his fingers into Reno's neck.

There was no pulse.

The Reno Kid was dead.

Finale

The sound of gunfire had ceased long before the sun had risen to announce a new day. Major Seth Provine had led Hal Cartwright and his valiant cowboys across the deadly desert. They had followed the outlaws' hoof tracks right to the six dead bodies and the secret wine cellar. They found Clu Marvin propped up against the strange brick archway. He had not moved far from the body of the man who had saved his life at the cost of his own.

Provine dropped from his grey and knelt beside the cowboy.

'Are you OK, Clu?'

'Got me a bullet in my back, but apart from that I'm doin' OK, Major,' Clu replied.

'What happened here?' Cartwright asked as he dismounted and stared at the bodies of the sheriff and Reno. 'Shoot-out?'

'The trail is littered with bodies, Clu,' the major added.

'Reno got 'em.' Marvin gestured toward the Kid.

'Is that the Reno Kid?' Cartwright gasped.

Clu nodded.

'Yep.'

'So it was him that was behind this all the time?' the deputy surmised.

Clu Marvin shook his head.

'You're wrong. He saved my bacon. Reno picked me up off the desert and brought me here. There's water inside here. That's the only reason I'm still alive.'

The major rubbed his chin.

'Reno killed all these folks?'

'Not all. It's a long story, I'll tell ya when I ain't so tuckered.' Clu smiled.

'Leastways it's all over now.' Cartwright smiled.

'Have ya arrested Lex Reason yet?'

Clu asked as two of the cowboys helped him to his feet.

'What for?' Provine asked curiously.

' 'Coz he's behind all the killin' ya see here, Major,' Clu replied. 'He had me a prisoner in that red house of his. He's the dude that shot me in my back when I escaped.'

'I always knew that fancy dude was no good!' The deputy sighed. 'Give me all the details, son.'

'I'll tell ya all about it on the way back to town.'

Able Jones rode up the gully and stopped his mount next to the major. He leaned down.

'What we gonna do with all these bodies, Major?'

Cartwright stepped forward.

'Tie them on to those horses we found. We got us a lot of reward money to calculate when we get back to McCoy.'

Clu Marvin shook his head.

'All this was caused by greedy folks wanting to get their grubby hands on reward money, Deputy. Kinda makes me feel sick.'

'Sick?' Cartwright raised both his eyebrows. 'By my reckoning all the reward money belongs to you, son. Every damn penny of it.'

The major rested a hand on the shoulder of the injured cowboy and whispered in his ear.

'You're right to feel sick, Clu. But Hal's correct. The reward money is rightly yours. None of us can lay claim to it.'

Clu Marvin went to Reno's faithful mount and ran a hand down its neck. The animal had not moved an inch away from its dead master since Reno had breathed his last.

'I'll just take this horse. Reno's horse.'

'But what of the reward money?' the deputy asked.

'The major will know what to do with that. Maybe buy some new breeding stock for the ranch.' Clu Marvin carefully mounted the horse and steadied it. ‘Heck, I’m just a cowboy.’

Provine looked up proudly and smiled.

‘A fine cowboy, Clu. A mighty fine cowboy.’

Other titles in the
Linford Western Library:

BADGE OF EVIL

Andrew Johnston

Lawyer Jack Langan left New York to travel out west to meet the father who had abandoned him. But he didn't expect to be offered the richest ranch in the territory — or imagine that he would be abducted. And he certainly could not have envisaged challenging the sheriff to a gunfight in front of an angry crowd of townspeople . . . For Langan to survive, he must discover his own courage and learn to understand the ways of the West.

BUZZARD'S BREED

David Bingley

When Jim Storme went to join his brother Red, and his cousin, Bart McGivern, in Wyoming, he was heading for trouble. Cattle barons were attacking lesser men, and branding them as rustlers . . . Jim joined the cattlemen's mercenaries, but he changed sides when confronted by his brother, Red. When a wagon loaded with dynamite hit their ranch, it was one of many clashes between settlers and invaders in which the three Texans made their mark, and struggled to survive.

'LUCKY' MONTANA

Clayton Nash

Sean Rafferty wanted money to buy back the ruins of his family's estate in Ireland. He didn't care how he got that money or how many lives he ruined in the process . . . A man called 'Lucky' Montana found that fate threw him into the deal. With a bounty hunter already stalking him, Montana now had to contend with Rafferty's murderous crew as well . . . Now he must stride into battle, knowing that there is always a bullet waiting for him.